My Invisible Naked Friend

F. Hampton Carmine

DEDICATION

I want to dedicate this story to everyone who is struggling to discover who they are, and to all those who help them.

ACKNOWLEDGMENTS

I want to thank my family for putting up with me during the writing of this story. Thanks to the Science Fiction and Fantasy Group of the Durham Writers Group for excellent and constructive feedback.

CONTENTS

CHAPTER ONE

Friday, November 2nd, had begun well for Darcy Marie Winters. She and three upperclassmen squad mates from cheer leading were eating lunch together at Santa Monica High. She had worked very hard since school started to reach the varsity cheer leading squad as a sophomore and almost dared to consider her companions as friends. She certainly felt honored that they had asked to sit with her.

Her pride at their company, however, began to erode almost from the beginning as the older students had talked quietly among themselves while they ate, including Darcy only minimally. She told herself that she didn't mind so much. She knew that breaking into the upper strati of her school was hard and she had remained patient, watching for opportunities to interject her wit into the conversation.

The serious downhill slide began when the other girl's conversation evolved into the topic of boys. At nearly the same time, her phone began vibrating on the table, silently blinking the word 'mom' at her. How embarrassing. She glanced at it briefly but looked back at her companions, ignoring the call. Maisie, the squad captain and social leader frowned at the interruption and placed her hand over Darcy's on the table. The friendly appearing action felt decidedly unfriendly and demanding.

"You going to get that?" Maisie's voice practically dripped with irritation.

Darcy fought her instinct to yank her hand back. She disliked being touched. Darcy could feel the demand, the control, the pecking order clarity in Maisie's touch. "No. It's okay. What were you guys saying?" Darcy kept her voice neutral even as she stole a second furtive glance at the phone and slowly pulled her hand free.

Her mother never called her during the day. Her job as the assistant manager at The Clothing Emporium in downtown Santa Monica left little time for anything but emergency calls. "Shit, Mom!" she thought. "Bad timing. Hope everything is alright."

Maisie chuckled. "We were saying that boys have just one thing on their minds, right Darcy?" Maisie looked straight at her and she jumped a little. *Why was she looking at me when she said that?*

"You got that right," one of the other girls said and playfully tweaked her breasts. "But a little touchy-feely is nice sometimes. Right Darcy?"

Darcy blanched white then blushed red in the blink of an eye. Now the conversation really had moved into her most uncomfortable area, body parts and nudity. Involuntarily, she replayed, in her mind, the social disaster that had created her near phobic level avoidance of anything involving nudity. She could still see and feel it like it had happened yesterday, though it had actually happened at summer camp, six years ago, when she was ten. As a tall ten year old, she had already developed breasts, and a camp prank had collapsed the shower with her in it. She had been forced her to run naked all the way back to her cabin, trying to hide her breasts while the whole camp laughed.

That stomach wrenching panic over nudity still affected her every day. Despite her issues with her body, she did have a boyfriend, an upperclassman. Her phone began vibrating again, flashing 'Mom, Mom, Mom'. She grabbed it off the table into her lap, out of sight.

"Why the pink face, Darcy? You embarrassed by these?" The girl squeezed her breasts again and they all laughed, except Darcy.

"I'm fine!" Darcy turned her face away from the display, unable to control her reaction and they all knew she wasn't fine. She almost began to

3

questioned her need to be part of this group, why she didn't just get up and leave, why she even wanted to be a cheer leader.

Maisie glanced at her watch. "How about we drive to the indoor pool after school today ... oh, wait. You still don't have your license yet ... do you, Darcy?"

"I already turned sixteen back in September ... just haven't taken the test yet. But I'll be taking it soon." The phone that had finally stopped vibrating in her lap started again immediately; 'MOM, MOM, MOM', pressuring her to answer.

Maisie shook her head 'no', and stood up. "Well, sorry Darcy. Maybe when you get your license. Now, for the real reason we stopped by to see you today." She paused for a moment, then placed her hand on Darcy's shoulder and squeezed, looking straight at her. "Robert asked me to talk with you. You know we]re friends and he'll be there at the pool. When we last talked, he seemed a bit peeved with you. He said you guys were just not getting on okay and asked me to tell you that he needed a change of scenery ... well, of girlfriends, actually. Sorry." But her voice didn't sound sorry and her hand felt heavy, almost painful. Darcy felt like the floor was sliding from under her and grabbed the sides of her chair.

Tori grinned as she got up and leaned over, whispering into Maisie's ear. They both laughed while Darcy slowly withered, emptiness filling her insides. Maisie looked at Darcy while listening to the Tori's whispering and then laughed even louder. "Robert said what? No, he didn't."

She reached down and patted Darcy's shoulder again. "Girl, you got to get over yourself. Got to put out a little to get ... well you know, a guy like Robert. Seems he told Tori here, that no matter how nice he was to you, or how much money he spent on your dates, he couldn't get his hand, even close to ... well you know where." They all laughed except Darcy.

The phone began to blink again, 'MOM!, MOM!, MOM!'. Darcy stared at Maisie. How could she say something like that about her, in public? How could they talk even about that, anywhere? That is so private? "That's none of your business." She managed a strangled response.

Georgia laughed. "Darcy, you won't even get dressed in the locker room with the other girls. It's a good thing you're into math and science cause you'll never have a boyfriend at this rate ... hell, you won't even be able to have a friend, boy or girl."

The rest got up giggling and left Darcy sitting with an uneaten lunch, a blinking phone, and impending tears. She grabbed her phone. "What? Mom!"

And her world changed.

"Your father has been transported to the

hospital. Get a cab and get there as soon as you can ... his time has come." Her mother hung up and Darcy stared at the her phone.

The event she had been fearing for the last three years had come. "Dad!" she hollered as she grabbed her bag and bolted from the cafeteria, ignoring the startled looks from the other students. She called a cab from her phone as she ran down the hall.

She had known this could happen at anytime. And even worse, she had known that it would definitely happen, eventually. But 'eventually' sounds so far away, until its here. The knowing, had still not prepared her for the actuality, or the hollow dread that began to fill her.

Her father's Duchenne Muscular Dystrophy had bound him to his bed at home, three years ago. There, he had lived by the grace of twenty-four hour nursing care and a fortune in machines that breathed, drank, and ate for him. Only his brain and eye muscles continued to work without machine or human support. Since Darcy had been thirteen, her father had been suffering through these final stages, alive only through the administrations of his nurses and machines. He was present in her house but absent from her life.

With her father buried alive in bed under a thicket of wires and tubes, it had just been Darcy and her mother against the world for the past three years. But, even before his move into life support, it had only been her mother, father, and her. Her father had always refused to talk of his family, even became angry at the very mention of his parents. The topic of grandparents, aunts, uncles, and cousins was just as totally off limits with her mother. Her questions had always been met with silent, sad, or mad faces depending on the day. No extended family, no father, and a workaholic mother, made her world a lonely place.

The cab ride to the hospital seemed to hit every light and traffic slow down. When she tried not to think about her father, she would see Robert laughing with those girls about his attempts to reach into her pants. "Damn," she shouted, drawing a startled glance from the cab driver.

Her mother caught her in an embrace as she ran into the emergency room from the cab. "Come on. I'll take you to see him."

Darcy saw the emergency department as through a fog and allowed her mother to drag her along like a small child, despite the fact that she was taller by several inches. Her mother stopped outside a curtained exam bay and turned Darcy toward her by her shoulders, staring intently into Darcy's eyes.

"Darcy, look at me. This is it. This is the time we always knew would come. Your dad loves you and me, but he is ready for his torment to be over.

He is perfectly clear in his mind and he is demanding that we pull the plug and let him go peacefully."

"No." Darcy said aloud but in her heart she knew it was time. He had suffered a long time. He deserved better and she hung her head in acceptance. "But why now, today? Why like this, like an emergency?"

"Because it is an emergency." Her mother frowned and stalled a moment as if taking time to construct an explanation. "Today, tomorrow, it's all the same to him. He needs to go now. It is his wish and we need to honor it."

"But why today?" Darcy demanded. "Why not tomorrow, or the next day?"

"He has his reasons," her mother said and hugged her. "He and I have already talked and made our plans ... and made our peace. Now he wants to see you before he goes ... just know he loves you and always has."

Her mother drew the curtain aside and hung back a little as they both walked to his bedside. For the first time in three years, Darcy saw her father without the knot of tubes that had lived on him like an alien invader. The only thing he had now was his breathing equipment and his eye-movement-activated speech device.

"Daddy." Darcy leaned over and hugged him, too numb to cry. She remembered how nearly every day for the past three years, she had stood at his door at least once, struggling with competing emotions. She had needed to go in and hug him but had also felt horrified by his condition and appearance. She would begin to cry and couldn't force herself into his room. Under that tangle of tubes and wires, he had only existed behind his eyes and they had been closed much of the time.

Now, she held his limp body in her hug for several seconds while she forced her tears away. No need to burden him any further with her guilt laden grief.

Her dad's eyes glistened and began to move. His speech device began to drone. "Darcy, my girl, don't cry. Please understand that this is for the best. I've lain in that bed now for three years, doing no good for anybody. It was torture for me ... and for you and your mother. My love for you and she, knows no bounds and will never end, but I must ... in death, I can finally do something important for my family; you, your mother ... and the others. I need release. I need peace. Please understand."

"I do Daddy. I do, but it's going to be ... "She swallowed her impending sobs. "I understand. I love you." She started to back away but his artificial voice began again.

"We made so many mistakes, you mother and I, together and individually. Help her fix our family, all of it. Please. I love you." The machine stopped speaking.

Darcy kissed him one last time and backed away, turning aside to hide her tears. She looked back at her mother just as a doctor walked into the treatment bay followed by two people, a man and a woman. The business suited male approached her mother. "Mrs. Winters, Mary Winters?"

"Yes." She faced the man.

"I am the hospital's chief legal council. Your husband has had his final wishes on file with this hospital for the last three years, and everything is in order. We have four recipients waiting. But it would allow everything to proceed more smoothly and help to remove any potential issues if you would also agree and sign."

Mary Winters walked to her husband's bed and held his face in her hands. "I love you with all my heart." She sighed controlling a sob. "I will make this happen just as you wished ... all of it."

His eyes blinked and Darcy swore she saw a smile, though she knew that couldn't happen. Her mother signed several sheets of papers for the hospital's legal protection and then grabbed Darcy. The doctor nodded solemnly at her father who's machine said, "I'm ready. Do it."

The doctor turned off the breathing machine.

Darcy's father moved his eyes around his speech device one last time and it spoke. "Thank you, all. Darcy, one day you'll understand the whole story of my life. I love you, Pookie ... Mookie ... Ta ..."

He closed his eyes and moved on. His death was verified by the doctor, and witnessed by the legal council. Darcy heard a gasp from the female, who had entered with the lawyer. She had remained standing at the back of the bay. Darcy stood, anchored in her Mother's arms, spent, a dried up leaf buffeted by the winds of her loss and grief. Her father's childhood nickname for her, Pookie, kept reverberating in her head.

CHAPTER TWO

Darcy looked at her mother, but she was staring straight ahead. Her dad hadn't called her Pookie since she had been ten years old, and had never called her Mookie. She and her mother held each other as they walked through the curtains to leave the treatment bay. Darcy noticed the woman still standing at the curtain. She was crying and gently caressed her mother's arm as they passed. Her mother did not respond to the obvious touch of compassion, but Darcy thought nothing more of it, as her own grief carried her thoughts away.

That evening, they began the process of preparing her father's personal items for donation according to his long standing wishes. The house was quiet, too quiet. The mechanical sounds that had poured from her father's room for the past three years, were missing. Darcy stared through the window of the spare bedroom that had been her father's in-home hospital room. She couldn't think about anything for more than a few seconds at a time. What was she supposed to do? What was supposed to happen now. She knew she should be supporting her mother who was also standing in the bedroom staring in the other direction, but she didn't have anything to give.

Darcy knew her father had previously arranged, that upon his death, the machines that had allowed him to live at home, were to be donated to the hospital respiratory therapy unit. He had been very explicit, he did not want Darcy or her mother to live with any constant reminders of him scattered around the house. His clothes and select personal items were to be donated to the homeless shelter as soon as possible, and his ashes given to the sea. No plot of soil and no urn of ashes on the mantle for them. But as they packed the boxes, Darcy couldn't bring herself to actually close them. If she could still see his belongings, he didn't seem to be quite as gone.

Slowly, Darcy would pack a box, pass it to her mother, and then feel guilty for leaving her to seal and label it. Between the tears, and the bouts of deep breathing while standing and staring, they spoke only of immediate things like cardboard boxes, tape, and magic markers. They never spoke of the missing presence in the room. Eventually, when neither of them could bring themselves to touch any more of his things, they moved to the living room, sat in front of the TV, and just hugged. Neither cared if it was even on, or what may have been playing.

After some period of time, her mother finally sighed, a great heaving of her chest, like something was over, like it was time to move on. "Are you okay? I know this was hard ... is hard. You had no warning at all. At least he and I had talked about his decision several times before today."

"You knew ... you knew before?" Darcy felt shocked but neither her expression or voice had enough energy to betray her feelings.

"We'd been discussing his desires for the past month, but today, ... things happened ... things developed and he said 'enough, it's time'." Darcy's mother sat up and faced her. "Even though we have had at least the last three years to prepare for ... for his passing, it is going to be a hard time for both of us for a while."

Her mother was right. Knowing, would not have helped much. "I'll be okay. I love you ... I guess it's just me and you now, against the world."

"That's right, just you and me, kid." Her mother got up. "Ah, one more thing, you should know. Tonight, just after midnight, they are going to harvest his organs for transplant donations. It was one of your father's strongest desires, to help others live when he died. Because of his choice ... at least four others may now have a new chance to live."

Organ donation made since. Darcy knew he would have wanted that. Her grief stricken, exhausted brain wasn't working or she would not have said what tumbled from her mouth next. "I know Dad would not talk of his family, or you either, about yours, but isn't now a good time to have more family around? Wouldn't they want to know ... that he is gone? Isn't there anyone that we need to notify or contact? Dad did say to help our family."

"No." Her mother didn't sound angry, just firm. "It's just me and you. We can't, shouldn't ... don't need to involve them."

"Them? So, there are others."

"Not ... to us ... not now." Her mother was very definite.

"Okay ... love you, Mom." No new news there, even in this difficult time.

"Love you too. I'm going to bed. Got to go to work tomorrow, nine to seven. You'll be okay, here by yourself, tomorrow?"

"You don't work Saturdays, usually."

"I need to work this one." Her mother looked away.

"Well, of course I'll be okay. I am sixteen." Darcy's voice projected a confidence she did not feel. The idea of being alone, now, was daunting.

Her mother smiled thinly and left the living room. Darcy tried to watch the movie but couldn't concentrate. Who was she now? Was she the same red haired, green eyed, five foot eight, sixteen year old sophomore in high school as before? No! Now, she was also fatherless, and nearly without family. At least she had her father's height, hair and eyes, and his love of math and science.

The more the thought about it, the more the feelings of guilt rose. She had felt fatherless for the last three years, since he had become bedridden. He had disappeared into that room under a gnarl of wires and tubes. He had technically been alive, but he had still been gone. As of today at lunch, she was boyfriend-less too. Asshole, talking to one of her friends behind her back just because she wouldn't put out.

Darcy slept fitfully that night, asleep and awake in equal amounts. She woke twice sensing a presence, like someone was standing by her bed, staring at her. Assuming that the silhouette was her worried mother, she drifted back to sleep, finally waking up after her mother had gone to work the next morning.

The house was silent, the constant sound of pushed air and the mechanical rhythms of her father's breathing machine were missing. She found that she needed that sound. She may have been too scared to go into his room when he had been there, but that sound had meant he was still alive. After flipping the switch on the machine, she hung her head and listened. Even on, it wasn't the same, it echoed differently in the now nearly empty room. She turned it back off.

She had to get out of the house but couldn't face any of her normal weekend hangouts where she could run into people she might know. The park would have to do. *Why didn't I take the driver's test earlier*, she thought as she stared at her bicycle. Sliding her hand along the crossbar, she recalled the birthday when she had gotten the bike. Oh well, she realized that she knew exactly why she had stalled on her driving test. With her hand on the seat, she remembered her thirteenth birthday and her father standing beside the bicycle, shaking on two canes, grinning. That was the last smile she could remember and that bike was the last gift he had given her before he disappeared into that room. She loved her bike.

The ride to the park was quiet, the city sounds forming a shield between her and the dark clouds of gloom and loneliness that surrounded her in her world. The park was quiet, open, and thankfully empty of visitors at this time of mid-morning. Standing her bike against one of the many vacant benches, she sat and leaned back with her eyes closed. She felt adrift in a sea of grief, at the mercy of the relentless waves of her own self pity that crashed over her, scattering her thoughts like wispy clumps of sea foam.

Suddenly she sensed a sound, or a movement, or maybe a presence and she opened her eyes. Out of the corner of her eye she saw a naked teenage girl sitting on the bench beside her, crying, the tears falling from her bowed head onto her breasts. When Darcy jerked her head around in shock, to look directly at her, there was no one there. Please, no! She was letting her grief push her into craziness, into seeing things. Her father had had to fight hallucinations too, toward the end. Seeing things was one thing but why naked? She shuddered.

She heard her name being called and suddenly Darcy's best friend, Roberta Cordoba, a bilingual Spanish and English speaking student from Mexico, skidded her bike to a halt in front of the bench. They shared a love of music and science, and Darcy was learning Spanish from her; helpful where she lived. "Roberta!"

"Thought you'd be here when you weren't home. Heard about your Dad, so sorry." She dropped her bike and sat beside Darcy, placing her hand on Darcy's shoulder but drew it back when Darcy flinched.

Darcy shook her head in resignation and briefly squeezed Roberta's hand. "Sorry, just a little defensive. We knew this would happen sometime, sooner or later. You know, he had been really sick since I was thirteen. He and Mom had felt it would be best to spend his remaining years at home. With his company's insurance, the machines, and twenty-four hour nursing, he did live for over three years. But I think he got tired of just existing in that bed. I think he wanted to go. Guess it's just Mom and me now ..."

"Are you and your mom going to be okay ... with money and all?"

"Yeah. Dad's life insurance will give us enough money to continue as we are now, as long as Mom works, but I think she needs to work anyway. I mean, she is always working."

"You sound awfully cool and calm. What gives?"

"Just numb." Darcy took a deep breath, realizing that in addition to her grief, she almost felt a sense of relief that she would no longer be alone in the house with her incapacitated father when her mother was at work; no longer have to avoid the doorway when the nurse was bathing him; no longer seeing his machines and not seeing him. She felt dirty, guilty, for even thinking like that. She looked up at Roberta, suddenly in tears. "How could he leave me? And how can I be mad at him for dying? What kind of horrible person am I anyway?"

She could see Roberta was crying now too and she wiped her tears. "Sorry for being such a wuss."

"My tears are not for you, well, not just for

you." Roberta stood up and briefly turned her back before facing Darcy again. "I know this is a terrible time to tell you this, but my visa has run out and ICE has told me to go back to Mexico peaceably. My family in Mexico City has arranged for me to return. I have to leave tomorrow."

First her father, then her boyfriend, now her best friend. Darcy hid her face in her hands and they cried together for a while. When Darcy got back home, her mother still wasn't back. She locked the doors, then shut the door to her father's room and made a bowl of cold cereal. This day had to end. She threw the bowl, unwashed into the sink and slumped upstairs. A long hot shower would feel good.

She closed the bathroom door, the glass shower door, and stripped, her back toward the large bathroom mirror. While in the shower, she made sure to keep her back to the door before soaping and scrubbing. She shook her head in disgust at her own behavior. She was such a prude, now a boyfriend-less prude. But she couldn't help it, not after summer camp that year. She could still hear the laughter as she ran, trying to cover her nakedness. She had hated the kids who did that to her, but she had hated her breasts even more. She had been the only one of her age with breasts. At the age of ten, they had felt like alien growths and she had despised them.

She dried herself thoroughly and wrapped up in her towel before going down the hall to her room, where she closed her door and slipped her nightgown over her head before she pulled away the towel from under it. *Jeez, I am nuts.* The house was locked. Her door was closed. She was alone in her own damn room! Sighing, she crawled into bed, smoothing down her gown around her legs so only her feet and ankles showed. Why? Her mind reeled.

Why was she so hung up over her body. There was nothing wrong with her body and she knew it academically, but emotionally, she got embarrassed even looking at herself in the mirror. Her mother was normally free about nudity, not self conscious about her body at all. But it was what it was, and she was who she was. She drifted to sleep.

CHAPTER THREE

The funeral on Monday was a simple affair following Darcy's father's written wishes; a closed casket viewing with a short eulogy by her mother, followed by a cremation. He didn't want her or her mother tied down to a plot of dirt. It had long been planned that within the first several weeks after his death, Darcy and her mother would make a trip to the ocean. There, they would release his ashes off the coast, into the California current, so he could travel around the world, something he always wished to do.

Darcy could never remember the rest of that day or the night that followed. She barely remembered Sunday, the day before, when they had taken some of her father's clothing to the shelter and arranged for the hospital to pick up the equipment later in the week.

Darcy's mother had left early on Tuesday morning saying she had to meet someone for breakfast before work. Her mother's unusual behavior didn't really register with Darcy at the time as she stared at her rapidly cooling microwave oatmeal, alone again. There was nothing for her to do but go to school, but that was something that Darcy couldn't bring herself to consider, even though her mother had dutifully gone to work.

She vegetated on the sofa, binge watching nearly every episode of a simplistic anime about a young orphaned girl with the face of a ten year old, the fighting skills of a master ninja warrior, and a large bouncy bosom. Sighing, she stretched and suddenly felt a presence beside her. She looked quickly and was surprised by that same naked teenage girl she had seen in the park, sitting on the sofa beside her.

"What the hell!" She jumped off the sofa but by the time she turned back to look, there was no one there, nothing, not a trace. Now she was frightened, being forcibly reminded of her father and his hallucinations where his monitors would begin to beep furiously and his eyes would jerk around and fill with tears. She turned off the TV in the middle of the show and went to bed, trying not to think about going nuts.

Even going to school had to be better than sitting around the house seeing imaginary naked people and she dragged herself to school on Wednesday, albeit very late. She had been spotted entering the school by a hall monitor and consequently began her Wednesday morning in the principal's office.

"Miss Winters, I know you have had a rough time with your father's passing. I am so sorry for your loss. These kind of stresses in the life of a young person can disrupt even the best of students, like yourself. And I am going to extend you some leeway because of that, but I expect you to try to get to school on time in the future. Just come straight here next time you find yourself late and I'll clear it with your teachers."

"Yes sir. I'll do better." Considering her sour mood, she couldn't take too much more kindhearted lecturing. He couldn't realize that all that niceness was so far removed from where she was in her head, the emotional dissonance was making her angry. She glanced across the chair beside her, toward the door, and screamed. That naked girl was sitting right there beside her in that chair.

"What was that?" The principal walked around his desk and offered a hand to help Darcy stand up. "You okay?"

She stood up and turned to look again at the chair. No naked girl, nothing. Shuddering, she decided not to tell him she was seeing invisible naked people. "Sorry, thought I saw a spider. Really hate 'em."

As the day progressed, she felt like she was swimming in a fog. She missed her name being called multiple times in class. All she could think about was the funeral, the flames of the cremation, and her hallucinations of a naked girl. Why naked of all things? Of course, if it was her own mind playing with her, it would know of her nearly pathological avoidance of nudity.

Was she trying to tell herself something. She wanted to scream or cry, but who would really understand what it would mean beyond its primal sound. Who would empathize with her phobia? No one. Everyone thought it was funny. Even her mother was mildly amused, but it was not humorous to her.

As she ambled toward the cafeteria for lunch, looking at the floor tiles, she slammed into the back of her ex-boyfriend Robert, as he was walking with Maisie, of all people. Robert and Maisie burst out laughing as she stumbled back trying to regain her balance. Robert turned to face her, grabbed his crotch, and rubbed it. "Whoa, girl! Did you miss me that much?"

Darcy looked up at his leering face. Maisie laughed and pointed at her. "Robert, your stuff is safe. She can't even look at herself naked!"

The hallway blossomed with laughter, but it was rage that bubbled up through Darcy. It blew away any control she may have had. She charged forward and kicked him on his shin, a strong soccer kick, screaming an inarticulate curse word that sounded more like a growl. She got a second kick in before she swung her backpack at Maisie's head, clocking her across the face. Maisie fell over Robert, bleeding from the nose.

A teacher grabbed Darcy just as she rared back, preparing to kick them some more while they lay on the floor, squirming away from her. She grinned as she was marched down the hall to the principal's office. That had felt good, best she had felt since her father's death. Assholes. She may be a fatherless prude, but she had a temper and she was in good shape. Taking the seat outside the office as directed, she began to cool down from the rage fueled high.

The possible outcomes of her actions swam across her mind. Her mother would be outraged of course, as she abhorred violence of any kind. She could get a suspension and have to stay home. Damn, she didn't want to have to stay alone in her empty house more than necessary either. She had really screwed up.

"Darcy Winters, the principal will see you now."

She tried to appear humble and chastened as she sat in one of the two chairs in front of the principal's desk, the same one as this morning. But she kept looking at the other chair, afraid the naked girl would appear again.

"Miss Winters. That chair in perfectly clean. There are no spiders. And I told you this morning that I'd advance you a little leeway but this is twice in here already today, and it's only lunch time." He sat down. "Explain yourself."

She sighed. "Robert, my ex-boyfriend, made a very crude gesture at me with his ..." She blushed. "His crotch. I got mad and kicked him."

"Twice, I hear, on the shins. Brought blood too. And the girl?"

"Maisie? She said ... something awful to me and laughed at me in front of everybody and I just saw red. I swung my backpack at her."

"Hit her, I hear. A very bloody nose, too." He leaned over his desk. "They both may have been crude, rude, and acted entirely outside the bounds of common decency, but it was only words and gestures. Your behavior was physical and had real impact. You injured them both. Maisie has demanded to be allowed to throw you off the cheerleader squad ... I told her just to move you to alternate for an indefinite time. You'll need to work your way back onto the active squad, understand?"

Darcy sat up straight. "That crap about 'sticks and stones' is, well ... crap. Words do hurt ... but yes. I understand." She took a deep breath. "Sorry about my outburst. Guess I'm short tempered lately. Can you let me tell my mother about this first before you contact her?"

"I will have to tell her. But I will wait till tomorrow to call. You have tonight. Don't forget. And I expect more control in the future. Understand? Oh, and don't forget this coming Saturday is a makeup day for the brush fires last month. We are in session."

"Yes sir." She looked down to locate the straps to her backpack and saw two bare feet in front of the other chair. Not again. She glanced up at the chair. There sat a naked teenage girl, her head laying forward on her chest as if asleep with everything else plainly on display. She blushed deeply and looked back at the principal who was now looking at her with concern.

Ignore it. Don't look. It's not really there. She picked up her backpack, shrugged into it, and paused. She couldn't prevent herself from looking back at the now thankfully empty chair once before quickly leaving the office.

Her mother didn't come home till after ten that night and went straight into her room and to bed. Darcy recognized that she had been crying and was still upset, definitely not in a mood to hear about Darcy's school troubles. Darcy barely got a 'good night' that night, or a 'good morning' the next day, for that matter.

Her mother rushed out early again to see her friend for breakfast before work. It was almost like living alone. Darcy needed to talk to someone, not her mother. She needed someone her own age who cared about her life, her feelings, and not like her asshole friends at school. She needed a real friend. She flopped down on the sofa and drifted toward sleep. She would just have to be late again today. School was the worst, lately anyway.

She awoke with a start. Someone was looking at her, but only her mother had a key to the house. She sat up and saw that same naked girl staring at her from beside her on the sofa. "Stop! Please. Go away. I'm not crazy!"

She squeezed her eyes closed for a moment and when she opened them, the girl was gone. It was too late in the day to even attempt school. She closed her eyes letting the tears leak and roll down her cheeks until she fell asleep again.

She awoke a second time with a start, someone was looking at her again. "Get away from me!" She shouted as she thrashed awake, knocking her cellphone off her lap.

"Darcy! Wake up!" Her mother was standing there looking down on her. "What's the matter with you? Did you skip school again today? I got a call today at work from your school principal. You didn't answer your phone and I had to leave work to come home, only to find you asleep on the sofa. I need an explanation, young lady."

"Whoa, Mom. Too many questions."

"Don't whoa me. Start talking." She sat down beside her.

Darcy rubbed the sleep from her eyes. "I had turned my phone off. Yesterday, some kid made some very rude gestures to me and I kicked him ... Robert."

"Your boyfriend?"

"Not anymore. The day ... Dad died, He SENT word that we were broke up by way of another girl because ... well, because I wouldn't put out." She blushed and lowered her face. "Yesterday he rubbed his crotch at me and everybody laughed. That's why I kicked him."

"That jerk. And I'm proud of you!" She leaned in and hugged her. "Maybe be less physical with your response, but what a colossal jerk."

"Mom, your the best. Thanks for understanding." And she meant it, but her mother was still frowning and obviously not done.

Mary reached over and placed her hand on Darcy's shoulder, softly, supportively. "The principal also said that he had noticed some strange behaviors, looking at things not there and being very jumpy. Are you sure you're really okay?"

She was not going to tell her mother about seeing a naked girl that wasn't there. The hallucinations would eventually go away, she hoped. "I have been kinda jumpy, you know, hearing sounds, seeing things out of the corner of my eyes. That kinda thing, that's all." She hugged her mother and changed topics. "Can we have pizza tonight?"

"Sure. Call it in and get it delivered. I'm too tired to go pick it up."

Darcy already felt a little better but as they ate their pizza in silence, she needed more than ever to talk about her hallucinations. How to start that conversation without falling out of the pot into the fire. "Mom, what did they say about dad's hallucinations? Was it ... his disease or just his failing health? Or what?"

Her mother looked up, a frown creasing her brow. "Why do you ask? Why now?"

"Just curious." Darcy hoped her expression was open enough not to expose her real fears.

"Okay," Her mother said. She licked her lips as if the answer was going to be difficult. "The doctors all felt it was primarily psychological ... from being trapped in his immobile body under a tangle of wires and tubes ... probably stemming from a desperate need to escape."

"You mean they were like nightmares."

"Sort of, but more real to him than a mere dream. Remember, he couldn't move in response." Mary closed her eyes and sighed. "And we only knew what he chose to tell us afterward through his speech device."

Darcy shook her head. That didn't help. Was

her life so bad she needed to escape? If so, how could a naked teenage girl help? She frowned and turned away for a moment. She was so tired of being alone, and she let her frustration direct her speech. "Mom? I'm always alone! Why are you so late most nights?" She was far more blunt than she had intended.

Her mother looked up and frowned. "I've been visiting with ... with a friend, who is really hurting right now. It is a terrible situation and only I can help. Sorry to be gone so much, but my work hours will get better when your father's life insurance finally pays out. That should help some with my time away."

Darcy accepted her mother's obviously redirected explanation and hugged her. "Soon, I hope. It's lonely around here. Its getting late and even though I slept most of the day, I'm going to hit the hay. Night."

CHAPTER FOUR

Darcy began her Friday morning early. This time, she had to get to school before classes started. She needed to attend the special before-school cheer leading practice for the game that evening. She understood that, even as an alternate, she was expected to practice with the rest and regaining her active status would require her to excel and impress the other cheer leaders. She ended the practice disappointed. Her strange sleep patterns for the past few days had left her tired and she didn't perform to her former level, impressing no one, especially not herself.

After practice, she took her school clothes into the curtained shower stall with her like she always did, and hung them up high on the shower curtain rod to keep them dry. While making sure the curtain was securely closed before stripping in the shower stall, she grimaced at her own behavior, but she couldn't help it. She just could not get undressed or dressed in the locker room, sitting her bare butt on a bench in front of the other girls, towel or no towel. The mere though of it made her blush and shudder.

She finished showering and rinsing her hair. When she reached to shut off the water, she saw that same naked girl standing in the back of her shower. With a startled scream, she jumped back, tangling herself in the shower curtain as she tried to run from the stall. The shower curtain tore loose from its rings, she knocked the shower head aside in her thrashing for balance, and she fell thrashing onto the wet floor of the locker room. She, along with the curtain, her school clothes, and the spray from the shower head lay in a wet tangled heap.

The whole locker room of girls ran in to see what was going on. They saw a naked Darcy floundering about on the floor, pointing back into her shower stall and hollering. "Help! Help, there's a naked girl in my shower!"

Trying unsuccessfully to wrap herself up in the shower curtain, she moaned and cried from the floor, blushing over every inch of her body. She sobbed from embarrassment as the whole locker room burst into laughter; summer camp, all over again. If she could have melted down the floor drain, she would have.

"OMG." Maisie said. "Call 911, there WAS a

naked girl in there! But it was you! You sick weirdo!" The laughing crowd slowly dispersed, talking about the 'crazy' girl squirming on the shower floor.

Darcy glared back into the shower, but it was empty, of course. She got up from the floor, gathered her wet clothes, and ran into another stall. There, she squatted behind the shower curtain, sobbing in frustration and humiliation. When the locker room was finally empty and silent once again, she stood up and stared at her sopping wet clothing.

She couldn't go to class, not after the shaming she had just experienced. Everything was falling apart, school, cheer leading, and her family. School seemed more than usually pointless, anyway. Everything seemed pointless, her whole life felt pointless. Her mother seemed to work all the time, now, even taking all the extra shifts available. They had only talked twice the whole week. Darcy felt hollow, lost, adrift on a sea of loneliness. On top of that, a naked girl that only she could see, kept appearing and disappearing at the worst times. Since her father's funeral, studying had become nearly impossible, she had missed all but one cheer leading practice, and had performed poorly in that one.

Images of that asshole Robert rubbing his crotch kept popping up in her mind. What was she going to do? She needed a friend, a real friend, just hers. She screamed once more for good measure, knowing there was no one to hear it this time. But it still felt good as she listened to it echo around the locker room.

As she donned her wet clothing, she pictured herself sliding down a wet hill toward a cesspool along with all the shit currently in her life. With each piece of wet clothing she tugged and stretched into place, Darcy cared less about the world around her, and less for herself. Finally dressed, but still dripping wet, she walked down the hallway from the gym.

She didn't care what she looked like. She didn't care what anyone who saw her thought as she gravitated toward the library, passing several students. After looking at her face and her bearing, they wisely moved silently aside. Grimacing, she realized that she must have appeared on the outside just like she felt on the inside.

Turning into the school library, she walked to her favorite area, the farthest table in the back next to a rarely used section of stacks, and sat. Her expression warned against conversation, daring anyone to even look in her direction. Stretching her arms out in front of her on the table, she laid her head on them, squeezing her eyes closed as tightly as she could. Maybe the world would go away if she kept them closed long enough. Class could go suck lint, she was not moving from this table.

Suddenly she felt that presence again, that same presence she had felt periodically over the past week. It was an assault to her solitude, and she looked up. There she was, that same naked girl, about her own age, but this time, she was sitting right beside her. The naked girl was laying forward over the table with her head on her arms, a mirror of Darcy herself. She had the same red hair and pale skin Darcy recalled from her previous appearances. Was it real memories or was the whole thing manufactured in her head?

This time, the girl didn't disappear, even when Darcy stared directly at her. This time, she just sat there in all her nakedness. Darcy's mouth began to work before her brain and she shouted at the naked girl. "Dammit! You've got to stop it! You can't be here, naked like that! Go away and leave me alone!"

The naked girl raised her head, her face stained from crying and her green eyes were rimmed in red. She looked confused as her red hair fell across her shocked expression. "You can see me?"

"Of course I can see you. You're sitting right there, stark naked!" Darcy looked at the floor, then the ceiling, then she held her palm out, blocking most of the girl from view. She carefully looked only at the girls eyes. The girl had really been crying. Her face was a mess. *My hallucination had been crying? What could that mean?* Darcy looked around the library, and the other students were all looking at her and whispering to each other.

"Where am I?" The girl ask.

"What?" Darcy asked in a hoarse whisper, trying not to draw any more attention to herself. Her hallucination asked a question. *No! Just stop it! Don't talk to your hallucination. Ignore it. It will go away.* But the girls desperate, lost expression pulled at her and she answered anyway. "You're in the school library."

"How did I get here?" The girl sat up and looked down at herself and her eyes went round in surprise as she gasped. "Shit! Where are my clothes?"

"How would I know?" Darcy couldn't stop responding. She stood up. "You got to stop following me around! And put on some damn clothes. What is the matter with you?" She heard giggling and hushed conversation from somewhere behind her in the stacks.

The girl looked up directly at Darcy. "Following you? You do look familiar ... who the hell are you? What is happening to me?" Tears began to flow again.

Darcy shook her head. She was carrying on a conversation with a naked girl in the school library, a naked girl most likely from her own imagination that no one else could see. But there was something in the girls eyes, a neediness, a loneliness, that drew a sympathetic response from Darcy despite the bizarre situation. "Jeez. Don't cry. Are you okay, injured, sick? *What am I doing? Stop talking to the invisible girl. She's not real.*

Ms. Tully, the librarian walked up. "Darcy, who are you talking to, so loudly?"

"Sorry. I don't know her name but..." Darcy pointed to the now empty chair beside her. The girl was gone, again. "She was right here!"

"Darcy, there was no one there. I've been watching now for several minutes. You sure you're okay?" She reached for her shoulder but Darcy ducked the friendly gesture.

Ms. Tully stepped back. "Darcy, I believe you need to talk to your mother and maybe a professional. Please go see the school nurse ... wait. Why are you soaking wet?"

"No nurse. I'm going home, and don't try to stop me." Darcy grabbed her backpack and fled the library, her mind's eye filled with an image of the naked girl's desperate, lonely expression. She could still hear her fellow students laughing at her, the crazy, fatherless, boyfriend-less girl. Darcy's mind raced around and around. Was she nuts. Were hallucinations hereditary? She recalled seeing a few of her father's periodic hallucinations and his terror afterwards.

When she finally reached the bus stop, two blocks down Pico, she flopped down on the bench to wait. Suddenly, she sensed that same presence she had felt in the library. The girl was back! The naked girl was sitting right beside her again, almost touching elbows. Darcy jumped over to the far end of the bench. "Damn. Where did you come from? Where did you go before?"

"I don't know and I don't know. Where am I now?" The girl sounded so lost and helpless, her voice pulled at Darcy's heart.

"The bus stop on Pico. What's your name?"

"I don't know."

"Well, why are you naked?"

"I don't know."

"Well, at least cover yourself, would you?"

"Am I ugly?"

"No, but you're completely naked."

Darcy turned away and ignored her for several minutes but finally glanced back toward her after hearing nothing the whole time. The girl was just sitting there with a confused, tearful expression like a little lost child. Darcy looked past her, above her, at the sidewalk, but all to no avail. All she could see was skin. In frustration, she asked again, "Why are you so damn naked? And why do you look like me?"

"You already asked me that and I still don't know. I do?" The girl never looked up.

"Sorry. But your nakedness is very embarrassing for me. You have no idea how much.

I don't know where to look. Can you at least cover yourself? Please."

The girl placed her hand over her crotch and an arm across her breasts. "How do you think I feel, out here like this?" She glared at Darcy. "Is this good enough for you?"

"Yeah, that helps a little."

""I'm so glad you're more comfortable." The girl shivered a little and looked up toward the morning sky.

Darcy looked closer at her; red hair, green eyes, fair skin, tall, and slender, and well developed. Oops. She had to look away.

Darcy watched the pedestrians walk by. They were avoiding looking at her, but had no reaction to the naked girl on the other end of the bench. She hung her head. Now, she knew for sure that only she could see the girl and grimaced, knowing what the passersby were thinking, because she was thinking the same thing. There was a crazy girl talking to herself as she waited for the bus.

No, not crazy. She thought. She was just imagining the girl. She looked over at her. "You don't exist! You're just a figment of my imagination. So, go away! My life is already screwed up enough. I don't need hallucinations too." She closed her eyes and waited for the girl to disappear. Instead, she heard the girl begin to cry and then just continue to quietly sup sup. She did not disappear. Darcy kept her eyes closed, willing the girl to disappear.

After a minute of softly crying, the girl said, "You know, that's just a horrible thing to say. That was so very mean. I am not an hallucination. I'm just ... very lost." Darcy opened her eyes in time to see the girl move her hands to her face to hide her tears, forcing Darcy to look skyward again to avoid the expanse of bare skin and her very obvious body parts.

Darcy felt bad for her. But how could she feel bad for a hallucination. "Jeez. Don't cry. You know that only I can see you. Everybody else out here just thinks I'm a nut, talking to myself. And I think they may be right."

A suited man stopped and frowned at her. "You need to get off those drugs, young lady. It's disgraceful at your age."

She gave him a two handed, one finger salute and he moved on, harrumphing. The girl on the bench, however, began to giggle. Darcy glared at the girl. "So that was funny, was it?"

"Yeah. Haven't laughed for a while, I think. Wait a minute. If they can't see me ... then why can you see me?"

"Well, the question is, am I really seeing you? Maybe you're just in here." She tapped her head. "Imaginary and not even real."

"Of course I'm real!" The girl said just as she began to take deep breaths like she was suffocating and her head drew back in a silent scream. She disappeared from the bench, just winked out, gone.

CHAPTER FIVE

Darcy boarded the public bus and rode home, frequently looking at the seat beside her for the naked girl, who did not reappear. After another lonely microwave meal and a quick shower, she wrapped her own long red hair in a towel and stepped toward the large counter and mirror of her bathroom. She needed the counter, but not the mirror, which she carefully avoided looking into. Bending over in front of the counter to let her long hair hang down, she began to towel dry it. She may have been standing there naked in front of the mirror, drying her hair, but she never looked up. She rarely looked at herself, only when absolutely necessary, and definitely not when she was naked.

"You know that's the hard way to do that with hair like ours. Don't you have a hairdryer?" That girl's voice shattered Darcy's privacy and she stood up in shock. Her hair hung in long damp strings in front of her face from under her hands and towel still up on her head. That same naked girl was sitting on the counter right in front of her, smiling. Darcy screamed.

"Darcy?" Her mother's voice came from downstairs. She must not have gone to work yet. "Are you alright?"

Darcy quickly whipped her towel from her hair and wrapped it around herself as she turned her back toward the girl. "What are you doing here, now? I'm naked ... again." She blushed over every inch of herself as she stepped to the closed bathroom door and shouted through it to her mother. "Sorry Mom. I'm okay. The school nurse thought I needed more rest and sent me home. Thought I saw a spider a minute ago."

"So I'm a spider now? First I'm imaginary, then I'm an hallucination, and now I'm a spider." The girl laughed a little. "You know, I've never seen somebody blush on their butt before."

Darcy spun around to face her. "Would you just stop! Don't look at me."

"We're both girls, no need to be embarrassed." She hopped down from the counter.

Darcy watched the girl land gracefully with her bouncing body parts. "OMG! Put something on, would you?"

"I don't have anything, sorry."

"Here," Darcy grabbed a towel from under the sink and held it out. "Wrap this around you, quick." The girl's hand passed right through it, like she was smoke.

"Damn! I am a ghost," the girl said as she dropped her hand down by her side.

"Well, ghost or not, you're still very naked and I'm not going to stand here having a conversation with a naked ghost … hell, with a naked anybody. You have got to go away. I'm going to bed."

Darcy walked out of the bathroom, leaving the ghost girl standing there. She walked directly to her dresser and yanked open her top drawer without looking into the mirror. After a quick brushing, she put her hair up in a high ponytail to sleep in and grabbed a clean nightgown from the drawer. She was so flustered that she dropped the towel, and shrugged into the nightgown, instead of her customary order of nightgown then towel.

She closed her eyes and tried to sense the girl's presence. Nothing. She sighed, grinning with relief, maybe the naked ghost was gone and she chanced a quick glance up into the dresser's mirror to verify it. She was not gone and Darcy spun around toward her bed. The girl was laying on her side, propped up on her elbow, laying on Darcy's bed, grinning at her. "You have a very athletic body. Do you play any sports?"

"Why are you looking at me? I'm not

comfortable being naked in front of people. Hell, I'm never naked in front of people. I don't even look at myself naked, and I really don't like seeing other people naked!" Darcy sighed and walked to the other side of the bed, looking anywhere except at the nakedness on her bed.

What was she going to do with an hallucination that followed her around and demanded conversations with her. Darcy pulled back the covers on her side and sat on the bed, her back to the girl. What was she going to do? The girl seemed nice, and naked or not, Darcy felt somehow drawn to her, sorry for her. She seemed lost and lonely. What would it hurt to talk with her, to answer the girl's questions. There certainly wasn't anyone else around to talk to.

With a deep sigh like her mother, she answered the ghost. "I'm a varsity cheerleader. Well, I was until recently, and I've been thinking of trying out for the soccer team."

Immediately, she had second thoughts. Why did she answer? Was her need for conversation so great? Was she so lonely, she'd even talk to an imaginary girl, a naked imaginary girl, a ghost? Was she that needy?

"Makes sense. You've got great, strong legs and nice tight butt. Now soccer, that's a real sport." The girl rolled onto her back and stretched just as Darcy turned and tried to lay down.

"Jeez! Don't do that. I can see everything." Darcy closed her eyes and finished laying down as far from the girl as possible before carefully pulling and smoothing her gown down so only her feet showed. "Tell me this. If you can't touch stuff, like that towel a minute ago, how are laying ON my bed?"

"I don't know. Why do you smooth your nightgown down like that?"

"I don't know ... always done it. Wait, I'm asking the questions here. Its my bed. Well, if you're going to be here with me, I've got to call you something. How about Jane, like in Jane Doe. My name is Darcy, Darcy Winters." She closed her eyes as she pulled the covers across her. "Jeez, I just named my hallucination and introduced myself to it. I am nuts."

Jane scowled as she rolled back to her side and propped her head on her hand. "I am not yours or anyone else's hallucination! And very funny about the name, but under the circumstances, it makes sense, I guess. Jane it is."

Darcy quickly turned off her light and rolled to her side facing away from Jane. "Night."

"Night, Darcy ... thank you for acknowledging me, for being here, for seeing me. You seeing and talking to me has really helped. I was feeling excruciatingly alone and totally lost. Being with you feels right."

Darcy drifted toward sleep with naked Jane laying on the bed beside her. She smiled in the dark with the realization that this was her first sleep over since she was about ten years old. They had stopped after that camp fiasco. A sleep over with a naked ghostly hallucination. *Yep, I'm nuts.*

Darcy woke in the dark to an urgent and concerned voice. "Darcy! Wake up Darcy! You were moaning and crying. You okay?"

"What time is it?" Darcy mumbled.

"It's the middle of the night, about three." Jane was still in bed with her.

Darcy focused her eyes and saw Jane facing her only a foot away, under the covers with her. She was too groggy to move. "Sorry, can't help it. My dad died only a week ago. Still having nightmares."

"I'm so sorry. Was he a good father?"

How was Jane under the covers? Darcy wondered sleepily before she answered. "Yes. He was a good man and I loved him. But he had been very sick for the past three years. And I guess we always knew he could go at any time, but it was still a shock."

"At least you had a father for most of your life. I never had a father."

"You remembered that?"

"I guess. Just a feeling really, not a memory with details. You okay now?" Jane reached over and brushed Darcy's sweaty hair from her eyes with her fingers.

Darcy felt Jane's hand on her face and hair, and the rush of pleasure it gave her made her realize just how lonely she had become over the last week. "Jane! I felt that. How?" She reached for Jane's hand but she disappeared before Darcy could grasp her hand.

"Damn!" What was happening to her? She guessed her life had finally slid on into that cesspool she had fantasized about and now she was truly hallucinating ... no, not hallucinating. She had a naked ghost haunting her. She tried to picture Jane in her mind as a crazy vengeful ghost harassing her, but she saw only a lost, lonely girl, desperate for connection with little or no memory of anything from her former life. She remembered the feeling when Jane had moved her hair from her face, and smiled. Well, maybe Jane was wasn't so bad after all. It was a dark lonely world, lately. Sleep came easier after thinking of Jane and the nightmares stayed away.

When Darcy stumbled into the kitchen for breakfast the next morning before school, her mother was already dressed for Saturday yard work and was cooking breakfast. Naked Jane was sitting at the table, grinning. She said, "Good morning, Darcy. Your mom still makes you breakfast. That's really cool. Sleep well?"

"Jeez. Please put on some damn clothes." She

forgot to whisper. "And yes, I slept surprisingly well, thanks."

Jane shrugged. "I have no control. It's just naked old me."

Darcy's mother looked back over her shoulder from the stove. "That's good dear. Glad you had a good night. What did you say about my clothes with that potty mouth of yours?"

"Sorry Mom. Not talking about you. Just thinking about the girl's locker room where there are some girls that just don't care, and walk around completely naked!" Darcy sighed, scowling at Jane. "Sorry about cursing."

Darcy's mother passed a plate of scrambled eggs and bacon to Darcy. "You still all twitchy about being naked? Thought that would have passed on by now with high school PE, showers, and all." She set her own plate down. "Be right back." She darted around the corner toward the bathroom.

Darcy looked at Jane. "Yes, my Mom still makes breakfast most mornings. Her name is Mary Winters and it's just been me and her for a long while, no other family." Jane nodded, looking as if she fully understood, then she pointed to the kitchen door and Darcy's mother, standing there, frowning at her.

"That's right. Just me and you." Darcy's mother sat down and sipped her coffee. "Sorry for last week. I know I have been working too much. I'm going to slow it down soon, but I just couldn't be in this house that much. I really didn't realize you would be here alone so much. I thought you'd be in school and that between school and cheer leading, you'd be out of the house much more than you have been. I'm sorry."

"Mom, I'm fine and I do understand." Darcy looked at her mother and realized that she wasn't just being nice. She did understand. Her mother had been suffering too. She glanced at Jane, who sat observing the conversation, sitting there like she was waiting for breakfast, a part of the family.

Family. Darcy smiled. It felt good to have more family in these lonely times. NO! She shook her head, not family, just a hallucination or a ghost. She looked at Jane, trying to see only her face and the good feelings generated by her presence wiped away her efforts to feel negative about Jane's presence.

Naked Jane sported a gentle smile as she looked back and forth between Darcy's mother and Darcy. "You know, you should tell her about your nightmares. She would like to know, I can see it in her expression. That kind of sharing is important with moms."

"How would you know? No, hush." She whispered as softly as she could but could see that her mother heard her anyway and Jane stuck out her tongue.

Her mother looked up at her with moist, concerned eyes and sighed before she set her fork down. "I got another call, yesterday, from the school. They want you to see a psychologist. I know a good one, a Dr. Alice Norman. She usually works with kids who have been traumatized by kidnapping or abandonment but since I know her, she would help us."

"A shrink?" Darcy said around a mouthful. "You're kidding."

"No. Not kidding. You have been reported at school several times talking to somebody who's not there. You've begun to miss classes and cheerleader practices. Your grades have slipped severely, even in math." Darcy's mother got up and walked around the table, stopping beside Darcy. "Now, please tell me how you really are."

Darcy looked at Jane with dread in her eyes. She didn't want to cry, didn't want to break down, not in front of her mother or her invisible friend. Her invisible friend. Wow, what a thought. Even if Jane was imaginary or a ghost, she felt like a friend now. She had a friend who had brushed her hair aside and helped her with a nightmare and who was sitting with vicarious tears in her eyes. She was, of course, still very naked.

Darcy hung her head. "Mom, I'm just not sleeping well, lots of nightmares about Dad, his illness, and his hallucinations. I really miss him. I mean, he was gone from my daily life for the last three years, but now I miss him. How strange is that. But, I'll be fine. I'll pull it together."

She hugged her mother around the waist and asked, "Dad was a good guy, right, a good man out there in the world, not just a good father to me."

Her mother pushed Darcy's arms off her waist and backed up a step. "What brought that up?"

"Just thinking, quite a lot lately, actually. I know so little about Dad, his family, or you, or your family. I don't know anything about my own extended family. And it's a little lonely, especially now."

Darcy's mother sat back down and drank several gulps of her coffee before sighing deeply, a trademark action."Our family, both sides, have a closet full of skeletons, a large walk-in closet full. We've always kept it locked ... but maybe it's time we begin to bring a few of those old bones out into the light. Maybe it's time for it not to be just me and you against the world."

Darcy looked at Jane and smiled. Her family already included a secret ghost. "What do you mean?" Darcy said as she looked from Jane to her mother. Jane's attention was on Darcy's mother as well.

"Your father ..." Darcy's mother began. "How do I say this? Well, he was always a good man and a good father to you ... and husband too, after you were born, except for one time before you were born."

"Mom. You mean he ... he had an affair? Why are you telling me this, why now? Neither you or Dad ever talked about your families or your lives before me. Is it just because I asked, or is something else going on?"

"No, not only because you asked." Darcy's mother paused in her talk to fix another cup of coffee. "Well, for one, your father's illness and death changed a number of things. I have been feeling that we need to start being truthful, especially now, for both our sake's ... and some others as well."

She got up with her cup and walked to the sink for a moment before turning around. Darcy looked at Jane, still sitting there in her birthday suit. She smiled back at Darcy, looking excited and interested.

Darcy's mother sat back down. "We never told you about the affair, because it was between he and I, a private matter, not related to he and you, or to me and you. While I was early pregnant with you, your father went on a business trip to Seattle with ... his assistant from his office. He was gone over a week ... and he played around. When he got back, he was crushed by guilt, so remorseful that he confessed. I forgave him, mostly. And he was the perfect husband and father ever since. He was a good and brave man and I loved him with all my heart, We had a great marriage after that. But, I guess he wasn't perfect, but neither was I ... no affairs, but I too, have made some serious mistakes that affected this family."

Darcy thought about that. Okay, he wasn't perfect but learned his lesson and became a better man. She looked at Jane and shrugged and Jane said. "We all make mistakes. I'm sorry he's not with you any more." Darcy shushed her.

"She can't hear me, only you can. But now she's really looking at you funny." Jane pointed at Darcy's mother.

Darcy looked away from Jane back toward her mother and blanched. Her mother was staring at her and the seemingly empty chair where Jane sat. "Mom, I ..."

"You ARE talking to imaginary people." Tears began to stream down her face. "That's what the principal said but I didn't believe him. Oh God, Darcy. I've been so self-absorbed I didn't notice you slipping down that slope."

"Mom! I'm not crazy. There's no slope. You'll see. Things will be better now. I was just at a very low point." Tears brimmed Darcy's eyes. "I'm going to school. Things will be better, you'll see." She ran toward the front door.

"Darcy!" Her mother shouted. "It's Saturday, no school."

"Makeup day from last month's brush fires."
She shouted back.

CHAPTER SIX

Darcy ran sobbing from the house toward the bus stop, hoping that no one would stop her and ask why she was crying. She had no way of explaining without digging herself deeper. She had left Jane back in the house but she'd just have to deal.

The bus was quiet and she tried to examine her life as she rode to school. What was she going to do about naked Jane, her ghost, her friend? *Hell, my only friend.* She closed her eyes and laid her head back on the seat and whispered to herself, "I wish naked Jane was here. I need to talk to someone."

"You got to stop calling me that. It's kinda gross and sounds a little sexy." Jane grinned sarcastically from the seat next to her.

"Jeez. Why are you always naked? And don't say that word, sexy." Darcy hung her head immediately, having forgotten to whisper, again.

She had to conquer her reactions, but they just popped out. The other passengers looked around at her and she tried to shrink, as she listened to the whispered comments about the crazy girl who must have slipped off the deep end. She promised herself not to look at or talk to Jane in public ever again.

Jane just giggled for a moment before her expression turned serious. "You know your mom is just worried about you. You seeing invisible people must be frightening to her."

"Frightening to her?" Darcy managed to whisper this time. "It's frightening to me ... how'd you know where I was?"

"I don't know. First I'm lost in ... a big gray nowhere, then I sense you off in the distance and poof, I'm with you or near you." Jane shrugged forcing Darcy to look away. "I heard you say you needed to talk. I assumed about your mom, and suddenly here I am."

"Yeah, she thinks I'm going nuts and wants me to see a shrink. I wonder sometimes, too."

"Well, what about me? Being invisible and naked is frightening and disturbing as hell to me too." Jane leaned back in the seat. "But, Miss Darcy Winters, I am not your hallucination. I know I exist separate from you. Cogito, ergo sum."

"Latin? You're quoting Latin to me?" Darcy laughed. "Well, I guess you must know yourself. Temet nosce."

They both laughed a moment and Darcy whispered, "This conversation alone should be proof enough. No self-respecting hallucination of mine would ever be spouting Latin." She giggled again. "Thanks, I needed that laugh."

Jane grinned. "You know, if you want to stay out of trouble about me, you need to control your reactions to my sudden appearances and my lack of clothing. Tell you what. I'll help you desensitize. Yes, I will." Then she giggled wickedly.

"Man, that sounds ominous, but you're right, nudity has been hard for me since I was ten."

"Where you abused?" Jane's expression clouded over with concern.

"No, nothing like that. A stupid summer camp prank just got out of hand. No one really tried to hurt me. They just didn't know the depth of my issues with my developing body back then … when I was already ... already had ... uh ... boo ... boobs, as a tall skinny ten year old."

"Even saying boobs is hard, huh?" Jane nodded. "We need to work on that and I have a plan. I'll help you learn to stay in control. Okay?" She finished with a wicked sounding chuckle.

Darcy looked at her. That laugh sounded like trouble by itself and for the rest of the morning, Jane trailed Darcy from class to class, sometimes assisting with her classwork and other times making faces and pointing to her various private places.

Darcy knew Jane was trying to force her to break her silence as a form of desensitization training, and she persevered.

Darcy was sure she alone knew how distracting it was to have a naked person standing beside you, making faces while you are solving math problems at the board, even if it was only you who could see them. Suddenly Jane grabbed her chest between her breasts and fell over, disappearing as she fell. It took everything Darcy had, not to react. Jane did not reappear right away and Darcy began to wonder if anything was wrong. Where does she go, when not with her? All Jane had said was that it was a great gray nothing space.

At lunch, a couple of the more friendly cheerleaders from the squad, briefly sat down with her. "We know you've had a rough time of it since your dad died. And we know the principal already told you about Maisie's desire to kick you off the team. This is not about the principal, and not about the problem between Maisie and you either. Since you've missed a fair number of practices, we all voted, the whole squad, to officially place you on alternate status until you get yourself straight. Mary Ellen has been put in your place on the active squad. This is really not related to any issue between you and Maisie. We all know that she can be a ... well, you know. Sorry. We hope you feel better soon."

The dismay Darcy felt was tempered by the fact that she really had missed the practice sessions and had not performed that well on the one practice she had managed to make. She just sat there, silent. Guess she would just have to make her way back onto active status with hard work just like the effort she had originally put out. The girls had not been mean, but she just didn't need any more downward sliding in her life. When it had seemed like an unfair attack by a vindictive Maisie, she could rail against the unfairness without guilt. But now, the responsibility fell squarely on her own shoulders. She had messed up and must pay the price.

Suddenly naked Jane was standing beside her hollering at the receding cheerleaders. "Get away from her, you lowlifes!"

Of course only Darcy could hear it. Darcy quickly turned toward her but Jane was so close that Darcy found herself staring right where Jane's panties should have been. "Ah, jeez. Move back please. Aren't you embarrassed with all that skin showing all the time?"

Jane laughed and a few other diners looked around at her. Darcy hung her head. "Why can't I just be quiet when you're around. You make me crazy." She whispered this time and kept her eyes closed.

Jane nodded sideways at the receding cheerleaders. "That was a terrible thing for them to do." She placed her hand on Darcy's shoulder and Darcy actually felt her supportive touch.

"Thanks. But I really did miss a number of practices. They were reasonable. How are you doing that, that touch?" Darcy said in a whisper

"I don't know."

Frustration suddenly blew through Darcy's reserve. "Well, damn it. What do you know? I'm changing your name to 'I don't know'." This whole thing was getting crazy. What was she going to do? Jane did not respond. Even her presence seemed missing. Had her outburst hurt Jane's feelings?

"Jane, I'm sorry, I didn't mean anything, really. Just ..." She chanced a glance up but Jane wasn't standing there. She was now seated at the table, fully dressed in a cute outfit, a school uniform. "Wow. Were you in a school that required uniforms?" She did whisper this time.

"Yeah, a private school. They were strict about these uniforms too. You're looking at the ugly thing right now. Wow, I'm not naked. I can't believe it!"

"Nice ... so you were in a private school. That should narrow things down a bit, and it's not ugly, just plain." Darcy stared at her. "If you're a ghost, then you're dead, right?"

"I guess, but I don't feel what I think being dead would feel like. I feel an awful amount of pain sometimes and loneliness ... you know, for a dead person."

"Speaking of pain. What happened this morning when you grabbed your chest and disappeared."

"I don't know ... don't remember that." She felt her chest looking puzzled. "Well, maybe something ... no, not really. Damn! I hate this shit! It's like I'm lost in Dante's limbo."

Darcy shook her head. "Sorry ... wait. You read Dante. What sort of school was it anyway?"

"A very selective, strict, and traditional school for girls only. They really pushed the math and science stuff and the classics. I liked the academic part, the uniforms, not so much." Jane smiled as she smoothed her skirt down.

"Real memories?"

"I guess. Sort of fuzzy and getting fuzzier, now"

"Never mind that. Look, can you come and go when you want?"

"No. I have no control."

"Where are you when you're not here?"

"I don't know. When I'm not here, I feel lost in a big nowhere, like I said. When I'm near you, I feel good, feels right, like I should be here with you." Her uniform disappeared. Naked again. "Otherwise, it's like I'm floating in a giant sea of grayness ... it's so scary and lonely."

Darcy sighed. "Right. You're not an hallucination, I accept that. That makes you a ghost, haunting me. So what did I ever do to you?" She laughed and looked to make sure Jane knew she was playing. "Let's skip the rest of school today and go home. We've got to try and figure you out. Come on."

Darcy left school, tired of being stared at and Jane followed. Luckily, her movement down the hall did not create any unwanted attention with the hallway traffic monitors this close to lunch time. They rode the public bus for most of the twelve blocks to Darcy's house in silence. Darcy didn't look at Jane in her efforts to control her reactions and avoid drawing attention to herself. About half way there, Darcy felt Jane grasp and hold her hand as it lay on her lap.

A friendly hand felt good right now and she looked over at Jane. She seemed so real, so solid, and, she sighed, so naked. Darcy smiled, looking straight ahead as fast as possible, and squeezed Jane's hand in return.

Darcy needed to talk to Jane. But in order to whisper, she had to look at her and lean in close. She sighed and turned her head toward Jane, trying to see only her face, and whispered. "You know, either I have to just accept that you will be with me most of the time, or we've got to somehow, find out who you were and then let you resolve whatever is keeping your spirit here so you can go on, move on, or whatever."

Jane frowned. "You know, I really don't feel dead. But I do feel like I come to life with you. I guess you awaken the zombie in me. Arrrrg." She grinned at her joke. "You got a computer? We can look around online and see what we can find on the internet."

Once inside her house, Darcy threw her backpack down by the entrance and went to the room set aside as an office. She hollered down the hall just in case. "Mom. Going to work on the big computer for a while. Need to do some research." There was no response. "Must still be at work," she commented to Jane. "That means we should have at least until dinnertime."

She opened the door but before she could enter, Jane touched her shoulder. "Darcy, look at the note on the phone table over there."

Darcy read it aloud. "Darcy, gone to visit my friend again. Be back after seven. Eat something healthy! Love you! Mom." She sighed and grunted in disgust. *Gone again, with that ... that friend. Well, I have my own friend now too, invisible, but still a friend.*

Darcy's dad had used the office often before he had become bedridden and her mother used it periodically, still. Darcy also used it for homework and online research when she needed a larger more powerful computer with a large monitor. "With Mom out of the house, we will have the house to ourselves until after seven tonight." She turned on the large desktop computer and watched as the various lights began to blink and the drives spun up.

Jane stared at the computer with wide eyes, and leaned over as she stood beside Darcy, placing her derriere next to Darcy's face. "Wow! This is a nice computer."

"Would you sit down, your butt is right beside my face." Darcy had to turned away.

"You mean this old thing." Jane wiggled her butt and laughed before sitting down.

"You're a smart ass! No pun intended." Darcy had to grin as she shook her head. She was arguing with an imaginary friend or maybe a ghost friend, but it felt good to banter with a friend. "So, let's start. Jane, when did you first appear, or die, or sense you were different, or become naked? What is your first memory?"

"The first thing I sensed was that I was in a lot of pain and floating a featureless gray void, but not sure if that is a real memory. When you saw me in the library was the first time I actually remember appearing anywhere and you were there. The greatest thing I have every felt was when you acknowledged my presence ... my very existence."

Darcy frowned. "I take it you don't remember the previous several times you appeared, then?"

"Several? Really? Was I awake when you saw me?"

"Well. Actually, you seemed to be asleep, or crying with your eyes closed, or staring down at something. You never looked up and never stayed more than a second." Darcy opened a spreadsheet and began a list of Jane's appearances. "So, nothing about the time in the park and the other short times before the library."

"Nothing. Don't remember them. But man, I like this computer. It's got eight gigs of RAM and eight gigs of video RAM on an independent high-end 4D graphics processor board. It should be great for playing games, even the more resource hungry ones. What you got on it? Got GTA version 5, or Hitman, or Crysis?"

"What?" Darcy looked over, careful to look only at Jane's eyes. They were gleaming with excitement. "How do you know about that stuff?"

"I don't know. It just pops into my head. Well, do you have those games?" She tentatively reached for the keyboard but her hand passed straight through it and the desk as well. Disappointment clouded her face for a moment.

Darcy pulled the keyboard closer. "Never played those games. Never even heard of Crysis. Just regular old Minecraft on here and of course my boring favorite, Freecell. Mostly, I just do math and science research. It's got a good fast internet connection, though, because of dad's work ... his former work." Darcy chanced another look at Jane.

She could see longing in her eyes. It was so obvious that she really wanted to touch the computer. "How old are you ... were you?"

"I don't know. You've seen me, all of me, how old did I look?"

"Maybe sixteen like me." She began to type what she was saying. "Let's see, red hair like me, green eyes like me, about the same height, about 5-8, and slender ... like me. Damn, we actually look so much alike, except you are well developed, if I remember right." She took a quick peek and blushed. "Yep! Well developed."

"Hey, look at yourself. You're endowed quite nicely yourself. My boobs arrived early for me too and I hated them at first too, for years, just like you. And stop moaning about my nudity, or I might just start getting real friendly." Jane sounded serious and Darcy had to look to make sure she was joking.

"Okay. Okay. Early boobs. A memory?" Darcy sighed. Even saying the word made her blush.

"I guess, but no details just feelings."

They searched for deaths of a female teenager of Jane's appearance within the past month and found nothing. "Maybe you died a while ago, and not recently. What's the latest iPhone model you remember?"

"Model X."

"Jeez, that's a very recent one." Darcy looked at Jane's frustrated expression and felt sorry for her.

Then suddenly Jane's expression turned to apprehension. "Oh oh. I don't feel so good, feel faint. I'm going, bye." She winked out of sight.

Darcy stared at the spot where Jane had been standing. Imaginary or ghost, it didn't matter. She felt better when Jane was with her. She tried another internet search for recently deceased teenage girls that had attended a private school but found nothing useful. Her mother called at seven saying that she had to stay out late to help her friend again and an hour later, Darcy went on to bed early.

When Darcy pulled back the covers, naked Jane was laying there sound asleep. Darcy climbed in and laid down beside her before smoothing out her nightgown. She could feel Jane's warmth beside her. How was that possible. She touched Jane's hair and it felt so real. She was going nuts. And she didn't know what to think about a naked girl in her bed with her. If it was all in her head, did she have a thing for girls? Was it wish fulfillment? Was it just an embarrassing random hallucination or was Jane a real ghost? But then why was she almost always naked. It was so confusing and completely embarrassing. One thing was for certain, she was so glad Jane had come into her life. She left her hand on Jane's hair as she drifted to sleep.

CHAPTER SEVEN

When Darcy awoke late on Sunday morning, she felt fully rested for the first time in over a week. She rolled onto her side, coming within inches of bumping noses with Jane who was also laying on her side, but wide awake, looking at her. "Hey, sleepy head."

"Morning. Sleep good?" Darcy said, feeling pleased that Jane was still there.

"Yeah. Feeling pretty good, actually." Jane replied, suddenly laying over the covers stretching.

"Jeez, here we go again with all that skin." Darcy stretched with her eyes closed, preparing to get up.

"Darcy, are you attracted to me?"

"What?" Darcy looked directly at Jane's face, her expression confused under double layers of blush. The first blush was because talking about sexual attraction was incredibly embarrassing, and the second blush was because she remembered wondering the same thing before she went to sleep.

"You heard me. Are you attracted to me?"

"Not really. Not into girls." Just talking about sex caused her to blushed so hard she felt hot. "Are you ... you know ... into girls?"

"I don't know, but I don't think so. I don't really feel sexually attracted to anything or anyone. My attraction to you ... that doesn't feel sexual, just ... I don't know. It's like I'm only real when I'm with you." Jane looked almost ready to cry and turned over with her back to Darcy.

"Well, I feel better when you're here too." Darcy sat up. "My boyfriend up and dumped me last week ... same day my dad died." *Why did I admit that?* "Not even in person, either. He told another girl to tell me, and she did it in public no less, all because I wouldn't let him touch me ... there."

"Your vajayjay?" Jane grinned as she said it.

"Yes, if you have to say it out loud, or my boobs. I just couldn't." Darcy couldn't stop blushing.

Jane rolled back over and sat up, looking mad. "That asshole. Well, maybe that explains a certain sadness I get from you." She stretched, arching her back and sticking out her chest. "Have you had sex yet?"

"Jeez! Jane." Darcy blushed hot again. "No! And NO again. I can't even talk about that ... that stuff, let alone do anything."

"Any good feelies. Any tongue action?"

"What a dirty mouth and mind you have! ... NO!" She should stop answering and get up. She had not had a conversation about sex since the birds and bees lecture, and never had this kind of conversation.

"A deep, hot kiss on the mouth that makes your toes curl?" Jane said feeling her own lips and looking wistful.

"No." Darcy hung her head. "But, I've wanted to so many times." She hadn't even wanted to admit that to herself, let alone out loud. Why had she told a ghost about that deep desire, a naked one at that?

"Wow. You sound so conflicted," Jane said but she wasn't smiling. She closed her eyes. "I'm trying to remember if I have ever been kissed and I don't know." She began to cry. "Surely, there was someone who loved me. I can't remember anyone from before."

Without thinking, Darcy reached over and hugged her, feeling her skin and her warmth under her hands and arms. She could feel Jane's hair as it brushed across her face. From Jane's expression, she felt the hug as well and closed her eyes but her tears continued for several moments. Darcy shook her head in frustration. "How can we feel each other like this but you can't even touch ... well, anything else?"

Jane smiled. "I don't know. But thanks. I haven't had a hug in long time either." She held her hand in front of her face, a look of alarm beginning to appear on her face, and she disappeared.

Darcy laid over on her back, sighing and stretching her arms over her head. Her nightgown had crawled up high on her thighs but she hadn't noticed. She was thinking about Jane. It was beyond nice to have a friend to talk with but she knew she had to solve the mystery of naked Jane. It wasn't fair to Jane to be so lost, so helpless.

She walked down to the home office in her nightgown and opened the spreadsheet file she and Jane had begun the day before. She continued to fill in the list of sighting occurrences with relevant data; when Jane appeared and what was happening at the time. She also included what she herself, had been thinking at the time, in case it was all in her head. Finally, she recorded how Jane was dressed, or not, and how and when she left. Next, she started a list of things that needed doing to get her own life back on track.

She started the list by writing down anything that occurred to her in a sequential free-association style. Her thoughts bounced around from Jane to herself to her lack of family to her mother and her mother's new friend, ending with wondering what they were doing for dinner.

She stuck her head out of the office door. "Hey Mom, are we going out for dinner tonight? I'm hungry for ..." She stopped in shock. Her mother had just sauntered by, nearly naked wearing only a short nightie, a pair of slippers, and a towel around her head. "Mom! You know how I feel about that much skin."

Her mother flipped up the back of her nightie with a chuckle, forcing Darcy to look at the ceiling. Her mother stopped and tugged the short nightgown back down around her before she turned around. "Look, the house is locked, the curtains closed. It's private, your not a little child any more, and besides we're both female. I thought you were getting over this nudity phobia of yours."

Darcy sighed and looked at her mother. She pictured Jane who didn't even have a short nightie. "Well, I am getting better. You just surprised me. What about dinner?"

"We need to deliver the rest of the boxes of your father's clothes to the homeless shelter today and do some grocery shopping. We've let the kitchen run almost bare. We can stop and eat on the way back from shopping. Seafood? Leave in two hours?"

"Great." Darcy didn't watch her mother climb the stairs. She grabbed a cold sandwich, a bottle of water, and returned to the office to work on her life improvement list.

The homeless shelter accepted the boxes gratefully, expressing their condolences again and Darcy managed not to cry, again. She hated that she kept giving away bits of her father even knowing it had been his wish. Next would come the machines, then his ashes, then what would she have left of him?

After a great early evening meal, Darcy felt better. She and her mother had had a great conversation and some private time, unusual in the past few weeks. But she still missed Jane. Where was she? She hadn't been gone this long since she had first appeared in the library. Darcy needed to talk about her father. She hung her head in the car, not even feeling the wind in her hair from her open window.

"Sweetie," her Mom patted her knee. "I need to drop you off at the house when we get there. That ... friend of mine needs me at the hospital. It's a very tough time and things have just gotten worse. You understand."

No, she didn't understand. She was tired of being alone and her mouth overran her brain. "Mom. Is this friend of yours a man?"

"Darcy!" Her mother glared at her for a moment, then looked away and remained silent as she drove for another five minutes before pulling the car into a gas station and parking it.

Darcy sat in her own silent pool of anxiety and guilt, waiting for her mother to respond or explode, she wasn't sure which. Before turning to Darcy, her mother closed her eyes and sighed, leaning her forehead on the steering wheel. When she finally opened her eyes, Darcy saw that they seemed more hurt than angry.

Her mother looked at her. "Apologize. I do not deserve what that question implies. And in any case, I am an adult and my friends are not your concern."

Darcy had gone too far in her anger and thoughtless speech and she knew it. "I'm sorry, Mom. That was rude of me and inconsiderate ..." Tears filled her eyes. "But I'm just so tired of being alone in that empty house. You don't know what it sounds like when I'm alone with Dad's machines turned off and the house is so quiet. It's horrible. We don't have any other family and you're always at work or with your ... your mysterious friend. What was I supposed to think? And I'm not that young, I understand about s... about s... about that stuff."

"Still can't say sex out loud, though. I see." Her mother's expression softened and Darcy saw tears develop in her eyes as she leaned over and kissed her forehead.

"Mom, I ..."

Darcy's mother heaved one of her customary deep sighs, ignoring Darcy's aborted utterance. "Well, you are sixteen and I guess the ways of the world are not unknown to you. No. My friend is a woman." Her mother restarted the car and drove back into the street toward home.

Darcy waited for more but her mother said nothing else until had Darcy exited the car and leaned back down to say goodbye through the car's passenger window. Her mother frowned for a moment. "Darcy, JoAnne is a dear friend ... and more, but I'm not having a sexual relationship with her, just so you know."

"Mom!" Darcy couldn't believe her mother would say such a thing out loud, even as part of a denial.

"Just thought you would want to know ... should know."

Darcy watched her drove off before she walked inside. That conversation had not gone how she had anticipated. As she tried to watch TV and fiddle around with her homework, the brief conversation with her mother repeatedly replayed in her thoughts. She gave up and went to bed early.

CHAPTER EIGHT

Jane did not reappear for five long days and though Darcy worried about her, and missed her presence, she also used those days to get up on time and go to school. That all she could do to honor her feelings for Jane. She went to cheer leading practice and studied for the drivers test, which she planned to take in a week or so. Though she went begrudgingly, she also took time to talk with the guidance counselor about her father's death.

The hardest thing she did was ignore the side glances and outright rude comments from fellow student who still remembered seeing her talk to an invisible person and hollering about nakedness the week before. She kept her head down, and her mouth closed, for the most part. Jane would have been proud of her and her mother was.

She and her mother ate dinner together Monday

and Wednesday evening, a rarity with her mother's work schedule, allowing more mother-daughter conversation than had happened in months. But she still missed Jane; naked Jane, her imaginary friend, the ghost that haunted her, or the hallucination that wouldn't go away. She needed to talk to her and even needed her occasional touch.

Thursday night as well, she and her mother sat at dinner together. Between bites, Darcy worked on the list of things to do to get her life in order, the one she had started a few days before. She sighed after rereading the list and then laughed out loud at the list's contents. Gulping, she realized that she had forgotten about her mother across the table watching her.

"What on Earth are you doing so studiously over there, my dear?" Mary Winters laughed as she gestured at the piece of paper in Darcy's hands.

"Just making a to-do list to get my life back on tract. No big deal." Darcy folded it and quickly tried to thrust it into a pocket. Out of sight, out of mind.

"Sounds interesting. Let me see."

Her slight of hand hadn't worked. Darcy shrank in her seat. She was still not out of the woods with the threatened shrink, but her mother was being far too nice and involved in her life right now, to upset her. So she sighed and handed it over, grimacing as her mother read it aloud.

Things to do:

1. Help Jane
2. Take the Driver's Test
3. Spread Dad's ashes
4. Help Jane
5. Get back on Active Cheering status
6. Help Jane
7. Be nicer to Mom, she suffered too
8. Help Jane
9. Help Jane

10. find out more about this mysterious JoAnne person

A little lopsided smile creased Mary's face and looked at Darcy with raised eyebrows. "I really appreciate number seven. Number ten sounds so very impersonal, and I'm guessing that helping Jane is the top priority." She handed the list back and sighed. "So, who's Jane?"

Darcy folded the list and tried to return a smile but only managed a grimace. She wasn't going to lie, completely. "Jane is my best friend since Dad died and she is really having a very tough time of it right now ... sort of like your friend JoAnne." She smiled, seeing Jane's face in her mind. *Jeez, I hope that when she isn't with me, that wherever she is, it's a good place.*

"I'd like to meet her." Her mother said, and Darcy looked up suddenly. Her mother's words seemed perfectly innocent on the surface, but Darcy read deeper meaning from her voice and her eyes.

Darcy could tell that her mother was wondering if Jane was her imaginary friend. *I'm not out of the woods yet, apparently.*

"Soon," Darcy said. "As soon as we solve a couple of problems. Okay?" Darcy looked at her mother with her best, serious but worried expression. She did not have to act much. She was truly worried for herself and for Jane.

"Don't wait too long. Some problems just get worse if not addressed. I know this for a fact. I want to help where I can. Okay?" Her mother nodded at her and rose, leaving the table for Darcy to clean.

"Sure, Mom," Darcy called after her. *Safe ... for another day, maybe.*

Friday morning, Jane was back, sitting at the breakfast table, grinning. Darcy ran over to the table and gave her a hug, her hands grasping Jane's bare back through her long hair before she even realized Jane was still naked. She heaved a deep sigh. She was not going to let a little skin get in the way of her relief. "Where have you been? It's been five days ... I was so worried ... really missed you." Darcy blushed and turned to the stove and started bringing out pans for breakfast.

"Five days! Wow." Jane walked over to Darcy and returned the hug. "I wish I had a sense of time passing, but when I'm gone from you, it's like I don't exist, just floating in grayness." Jane looked around the kitchen as she walked back to her chair at the table. "Hey, looks like your mom is running late. Why not cook breakfast for her. That would be a cool thing to do. I know she'd really appreciate it. We all need to be nice to our moms."

"Good idea. But you'd better stay over there. Bacon spits and with all that exposed skin, you'll get burned." Then she looked up and grinned. "Oh yeah, I forgot. Right through you. Wait. Do you remember your mom?"

Jane sat back down at the table and concentrated on grabbing the salt shaker. "Not specifically, just get a good feeling when I think about mothers." Her hand repeatedly passed through the shaker. "Damn! I still can't touch anything but you."

"Language, darling." Darcy grinned as she broke the eggs.

"Yes, mother dearest." Jane quipped in response and they both laughed.

Darcy faced Jane with her hands on her hips. "That's bizarre, your touching stuff. On the one hand, you can sit on that chair and walk on the floor and touch me. On the other hand, you can't touch that salt shaker. You are a mystery."

After ten minutes of cooking, Darcy made up the plates and called upstairs. "Hey Mom! I made breakfast for us. Do want toast, too?"

"Oh, thank you, sweetie. Yes, please. I'm so late. Overslept." Her mother's voice floated down from upstairs.

Within a minute, Mary ran in, hopping on one foot while pulling on her last shoe and sat down at her usual place. Darcy noticed two things simultaneously, the plate of food that was sitting in front of Jane and her mother noticing that same extra plate. She had set three plates on the table without thinking. Her mother didn't say anything but her eyes narrowed with concern as she looked at the plate in front of the apparently empty chair.

Darcy blanched. She had slipped up again. "Damn. Sorry Mom, just in a hurry and wasn't thinking."

Jane looked enviously at the food and laughed. "Man, I wish I could eat it. It looks so good."

Darcy grimaced and shook her head at Jane but left the plate where it was. After sitting down to eat, she pointedly ignoring the empty chair and plate of food. She and her mother exchanged glances a few times between bites until Mary set her fork down and looked at her watch. "How's school going this week. Still going well?"

Darcy appreciated the move to a safe conversation topic. "As a matter of fact, yes. I have been very diligent in class and kept my mouth shut even ..." She stole a glance at Jane who was staring straight at her and holding up her breasts and making kissing motions with her mouth. Darcy's voice took on a hard edge. "Even when others were baiting me!" Darcy's eyes bulged and she clamped her mouth shut as she forced herself to look away. She heard Jane burst out laughing and she studied her plate even harder, trying to ignore her. Except for several hopefully unseen glances at Jane's continued antics, she succeeded, until her mother cleared her throat and Darcy heard her lay her fork down.

"Well, I'm glad things are better." Her mother pointedly looked at the chair, where, from the corner of her eye, Darcy could still see Jane making rude gestures. Then Mary took her finished dishes to the sink. "I've decided to cut back a little at work ... and I still know that very good psychologist, if you need to talk to someone."

"Mom! I don't need a shrink," Darcy said louder than needed, then sighed. She got up with her own dishes and walked around, very close behind the clowning Jane. As she walked passed her, she leaned in close and hissed, "What I really need is an DAMNED EXORCIST!" But she wasn't quiet enough.

"What was that dear?" Her mother asked as she turned back from the sink.

"I've got this, Mom. I really am getting things in order."

"Just worried, Dear. Thanks for breakfast. That was great." She grabbed her purse and walked swiftly out the door, her expression anything but happy.

Darcy spun toward Jane with her hands on her hips. "You little shit. No wonder I'm always in trouble. That wasn't funny."

"Oh yes it was." Jane stood up. "You should have seen your face. I thought your eyes were going to pop out!" She walked past Darcy and swatted her bottom, whack.

"Ow! I felt that, you pervert."

"Ha! Betcha no hallucination can do that! Let's get to school. Feeling good, and I anticipate a very interesting day ahead."

Oh Jeez, Darcy thought as they headed for the bus stop. She had been ready for school; homework done, a good breakfast, and dressed well. But now, she had her smart ass invisible naked best friend in tow. What could possible go wrong? She refused to think of all the possibilities.

Between English and Geometry, she heard her name on the PA system. "Darcy Winters. Please report to the guidance counselor's office." She looked around at the grins and smug expressions of her classmates as left her classroom and clumped down the hall to the office. She couldn't stay serious, though, because Jane was walking behind her giving everyone they passed the finger. By the time she walked into the office, she was smiling again.

"Hey, Darcy," The counselor said from her

desk. "How have you been since we talked last? You do remember that we also talked right after your father's death and also last week? We spoke mostly about your father, though, not you."

"I remember, Ms. Carlyle."

"I understand you've had a rough couple of weeks. I now have reports from most of your teachers, the librarian, and your cheer squad captain."

Darcy swallowed and looked over at Jane, sitting beside her in the other chair. "Yes, that first week was bad, and I messed up pretty bad. But I'm beginning to pull it together, really. I've kept it together all this week, at least."

Jane smiled and nodded. "Tell her about talking with your Mom this morning and her promise."

Darcy managed not to look at Jane but followed her advice. "I've been talking a lot more with my Mom lately and she's going to be home more. I've been studying real hard for the past few days and going to cheer leading practice. I'll get back on active status soon, I hope." She smiled, knowing that everything she said was literally true.

Jane nodded in support and patted her hand as it lay on the armrest. Darcy briefly glanced at Jane and smiled in response to the support before looking at their hands. Then she noticed the counselor's eyes also focused on the empty chair and armrest. How was she going to explain looking at a chair, filled with nothing, nothing visible to others, but she needed to try.

"In my worse days, I was afraid I had begun to hallucinate like my dad did toward the end. But I wasn't. I realized that I was just lonely and had started pretending I had a friend like I had when I was a little girl. I know it's silly but, actually, it really helped. But I guess I need to break the habit now. It's making my current social life difficult."

The counselor nodded. "As long as you're aware of what you're doing and know the difference between real and imaginary, you'll be fine." She got up and so did Darcy. "We can talk anytime you need to, you know that, right?"

"Yes ma'am." Darcy looked at Jane and nodded. "Come on." Then she smiled at the counselor. "Just joking."

Jane laughed out loud. "Damn girl, what a smart ass. Wish I could be that cheeky."

"Cheeky?" Darcy laughed. "You from England now?" The halls were empty, classes having already started, and Darcy spoke aloud. "And what are you talking about? Wasn't it you who was holding her boobs this morning trying to get me in trouble?"

"Yeah, that was kinda out there, wasn't it?" She held her hands in front of her boobs. "To here, even."

"Jeez," Darcy turned away and walked into geometry.

Jane helped her with several problems, demonstrating advanced skills at math, but she didn't know how she knew the processes. Darcy studied for the driver's test on the way home on the bus and Jane quizzed her. Darcy drew some looks from the other bus passengers as she worked to remember the California driving rules and practice test questions. She appeared to talk and repeat everything to herself. The other passengers around her seemed to understand. *Well, actually to misunderstand, but that works for me.*

That night, Darcy fed herself from cold leftovers and a bag of white cheddar popcorn while she repeatedly bemoaned her lack of an extended family until Jane jumped up, red faced. "Enough already."

Darcy realized that she had not been paying attention to Jane while she had been expounding. "I'm sorry. We don't need to talk about my lack of family."

"At least you have a mother and had a father ... I never had a father and I don't remember anyone else either." Jane sighed deeply and slumped a little. "Sorry. Not your fault. It's just that I don't remember a family at all. I guess I had one ... once ... must have."

"Well, I'm tired. Going to take a shower. Maybe we can talk about something else when I'm done." Darcy got up and went upstairs to the her bathroom.

She shut the door as she routinely did and a few minutes later, Darcy walked into her bedroom from the shower with her towel around her nearly dry hair. She finished drying her hair with the towel before pulling on her nightgown and had just begun to brush her hair, when Jane spoke up from the bed. "Hey Darcy, two things."

"What?" Darcy continued to brush her hair with her back turned toward the bed where Jane lay.

"You know that sometimes I'm under the covers and sometimes I'm over the covers in all my glory, right?"

"Yeah, no control, right?" Darcy began putting her hair up for night.

"Right. Answer me this. Am I laying naked in plain view right now? Don't look."

"Uh, I don't know. I didn't notice." Darcy smiled to herself. She really hadn't noticed. "Hmm. I guess I'm getting used to all that skin." She finished her ponytail.

"And second," Jane said with a knowing nod. "You realize that you just walked in here, yourself, naked as a damn jaybird."

Darcy looked up into the mirror at Jane, naked on the bed, and realized that she had been comfortable enough to make that nude walk from the bathroom down the hall to her room. "You're right. I didn't even think about it. Wow."

By the time Darcy reached the bed, Jane was under the covers, and Darcy slid under the covers on her side. "Jane, how do you do that with the covers? No, never mind. You don't know, right?"

"Right." Jane rolled to face Darcy. "You know, I never got to have sleep overs when I was little. This is kind of a treat for me, like having a family, like you're my family. Night Darcy."

Jane was right. It felt like family and it felt good. "Night Jane. Sleep tight."

CHAPTER NINE

Darcy woke up Saturday morning feeling like a new person. She stretched languidly and looked over at Jane, surprisingly still present and sleeping peacefully under the covers. Smiling, she eased herself from the bed. Staying in her nightgown, she quietly left the bedroom and walked downstairs. She did not want to wake Jane from what had appeared to be a very restful slumber. Jane would reappear whenever she wanted to, or had to, or could.

Her mother had prepared an a-la-cart biscuit breakfast this morning, with the many ingredients and choices laid out along the counter; bacon, sausage, cheese, lettuce, tomato, white gravy, and two kinds of mustard. Her mouth watered. She kissed her Mom on the cheek as she went by gathering her food and sat at the table in her normal place. "This is great! Morning Mom. How are you this very fine morning."

"You sure are annoyingly chipper this morning," her mother scowled at her over the rim of her coffee cup.

"I slept very well last night ... but you look a little worse for wear. You okay?" Darcy frowned a little in concern.

"My friend JoAnne needed a lot of support last night. It was very late when I got in." Mary got up to get another cup of coffee.

Darcy stole a quick glance toward the chair where Jane usually sat and sighed before beginning to eat. When she looked up, her mother was staring at her. "What?" Darcy asked defensively.

Her mother sat back and cleared her throat. "Darcy. I've held my comments for days now waiting for you to come to me and talk about Jane ... enough. I want the truth. When you look at that chair, like you were just doing, are you seeing someone?" Her voice was soft with dread and her eyes held impending tears.

"No," Darcy said drawing out her response. Her mother's expression broke her heart. "I don't see anyone ... now." *How can I explain?*

"Please Darcy, I need to know. Are you seeing invisible people like they say? Please, you can talk to me." Tears began pooling in her mother's eyes waiting for an excuse to fall.

Darcy hated seeing her mother so upset and was suddenly looking at her through her own blurry eyes. She didn't want to lie. She didn't want to hurt her mother. She didn't want to deny the existence of her best friend either. Her choices felt untenable!

She gulped and sat back down in her chair. "Mom, remember when I was little, maybe four or five, and I had an imaginary friend ... well this is sort of like that ... but not quite." She put her biscuit down and took a deep breath. Her mother deserved the truth.

"Yes, sometimes I see an invisible girl. Not people, always the same girl, just one; one teenage girl, my age. And talking to my invisible friend has really helped me. Things have been difficult lately but I'm not crazy, Mom. I know what's happening, what's real." Darcy hung her head. That was not precisely true. She didn't know what was happening with Jane. She did know that Jane was real though.

Darcy's mother got up, rounded the table, and grabbed Darcy up from her chair in an embrace, shuddering with worry. "With your dad's death and JoAnne's ... problem, well, I just couldn't deal with loosing you too."

"Mom, your not going to loose me. I'm going to be fine." Darcy sat back down.

Her mom walked by Jane's usual chair and looked at it for a moment before resuming her seat. "I've made arrangements for a boat at Marina del

Ray to take us out to release your father's ashes today. We need to leave about two, this afternoon, say, in about three hours. Okay?" She got up and went into the living room to watch what was left of her weekend morning news shows.

"So, only a few hours before the final goodbye." Darcy said to the now empty kitchen. She wiped moisture from her eyes and looked over to the chair where Jane usually sat, realizing that she had become accustomed to her presence and especially their banter. She also treasured the times she and Jane talked seriously. Jane had truly become her best friend and confidant. She needed her now more than ever, needed her support to spread her Father's ashes and say that final goodbye.

Sighing deeply, she cleared the table, put away the food, and walked into the living room thinking she would watch TV with her mother while waiting for Jane to wake up, but stopped at the archway and stared. Jane was sitting on the sofa beside her mother who had fallen sound asleep. Having Jane appear somewhere away from her seemed unusual.

"Hey Darcy. I've been looking at your mom and you know, she looks familiar." Jane shrugged. "Why would that be? She doesn't look like you. In fact, you and I look closer than you and her do."

Darcy walked in and shrugged. "Well of course. You've seen her almost every day now for over a week."

"No. I mean familiar from somewhere else. Like I had seen her picture ... before all this." She gestured at herself.

"How?" Darcy shrugged. "I'm going upstairs. I want to show you my collected diary entries about your appearances ... I finished them up the other day. But we need to do it now, before we go spread my fathers ashes in the Pacific this afternoon. I need you with me for that. Okay?"

She knew Jane would just reappear upstairs and walked away. When Darcy got to her desk in her room, Jane was already there, sitting on the bed. Darcy grabbed her laptop and sat on the bed next to her, opening the laptop to the spreadsheet she had finished earlier and then copied to a USB drive.

As they read the entries from the spreadsheet, they leaned against each other. Darcy clicked through the pages and they took turns reading from the screen until Jane sat up straight, frowning. "Wow! When you say it over and over again like that, being naked sounds so much more, uh, weird, but I don't feel naked. You know, embarrassed, shy, etc. It's like, well ... it's just me."

"Yep. That's you, my naked Jane." Darcy chuckled as she closed the file.

"Hey," Jane said, looking down at her arms and crossed legs. "Do I have any scars or marks that might help provide additional identification in our searches?"

Darcy frowned at her. "I've seen every naked inch of you, never noticed any scars."

"Well, naked or not, maybe my ghost form doesn't always show marks and scars. At least look." Jane scowled and smiled at the same time. "Besides, you don't see every inch of me. You've gotten real good at not looking anywhere but my face."

Darcy hung her head. "I know. I wish I could ratchet down my reaction to nudity in general, my own and others, but I've never had much luck ... until lately. You do seem to be desensitizing me quite a bit, though."

Jane grinned like an imp. "And remember, this sizzling body sitting beside you, may not be what my real body even looks like. I don't remember." Jane jumped off the bed and stood with her back to Darcy, her hands out to the sides. "Look closely."

"Sizzling? You wish!" Darcy laughed and then grinned. She had participated in a sexual joke. Wow. "Okay, I'll look. But you're going to really owe me. This is still difficult for me ... smack in the center of my weakest area."

Darcy sighed and stood up and began to examine Jane closely, starting from her upper back. She scanned Jane's shoulders and back, finding nothing. She knelt down and took a few shuddered deep breaths before checking Jane's lower back and posterior and then the back of her legs. Grasping

Jane by the hips, she turned her around. She felt the smooth skin of her hips as she grasped them. Touch worked most of the time between them now. As Jane slowly turned, her front side rotated directly into Darcy's face. Darcy turned her head to the side and closed her eyes. "Would you cover that up." Her voice was calm but almost dripping with exasperation.

"Cover what up?" Jane said, stifling a laugh.

"You know damn well what. Your vajayjay."

Jane laughed this time. "Wow. You actually said the word ... but why? You got one."

"Yeah, but I don't go around looking at it this close."

They both laughed but Jane still did not cover up. Darcy sighed and checked her legs and lower abdomen. She stood up, seeing no marks of any kind on Jane's abdomen, chest or breasts. "Nothing. A smooth as a baby's behind, like the day you were born."

"Well, surgery doesn't ring any bells for me, anyway." Suddenly she was wrapped in bandages and in a hospital gown.

"Hey, you do have some control." Darcy pointed at her. "You're not naked ... for the first time!"

"That's not control. It just happened. Wow. Maybe, because either you or me, was thinking about it." The bandages faded and she was naked again. "Well that was anti-climatic."

"Darcy." Her mother called from down stairs. We need to leave in half an hour, finish getting ready. Dress for warm weather but bring something to cover up with, to protect from the sun and wind out on the water ... oh, and grab some snacks from the fridge, in case we get hungry out on the water."

"Okay Mom!" Darcy turned toward her dresser and began rummaging through her drawers. Looking back over her shoulder, and smiled. "You sure you just don't just like being naked." Darcy said as she stripped to her underwear and pulled on shorts and a pullover.

"Oh yeah. Love naked." Jane began to dance and gyrate suggestively and moan. "oooooh."

"Jeez." Darcy turned away blushing deep red and walked out the door. "You coming, my sizzling sister?"

Darcy sat in the front passenger seat beside her mother while Jane sat in the back grooving, while the wind from Darcy's open window whipped her hair around. Darcy grinned in amazement. How was that happening? But she couldn't ask her, couldn't even look into the back seat, without alerting her mother. So she just kept grinning and looked ahead. "Mom, I've been studying for the driver's test. I should be ready in a few days. Are you off any days next week? You'll need to drive me there, to the testing site ... and I'll need a car to use."

"Good for you. It's about time." Darcy's mother smiled but kept her eyes on the road. "Yeah, I'll be off next Thursday. We can do it then. Don't forget to schedule it with the DMV."

It was good to see her mother smile and for the next twenty minutes or so, they talked of many things. Darcy mentioned the possibility of getting a part time job for the summer at the same clothing store where her mother worked and saving toward a used car. They discussed school, her ex-boyfriend, and playing soccer in the spring.

It had been a while since they had had such a calm conversation and it felt fantastic. Darcy smiled and closed her eyes, laying her head back against the seat, reveling in the moment and she realized, with a start, that they had not talked, even once, about Jane or JoAnne.

Jeez, Jane! Jane had been totally quiet for way longer than usual. *Jeez. Jane.* Darcy's' eyes popped open and she chanced a glance into the back seat. Jane seemed asleep and Darcy surreptitiously reached over the seat and poked her leg. Jane's eyes popped open and Darcy mouthed, "You okay?"

"Yeah, but I feel sorta funny. Weird. Thin even." Her eyes closed and her head lolled back again.

Darcy patted her leg and whispered. "Hang in there. We got a boat ride coming up. It'll be fun. I need you with me for this." Jane smiled thinly and closed her eyes. Something wasn't right and Darcy was worried.

"Darcy? Everything okay?" Her mother said glancing at her from the side. "She's back. Isn't she? Jane, your invisible friend?"

"It's okay, Mom." Darcy brought her arm back over the seat.

"I heard you whispering. Tell me the truth." Mary said, her voice soft with concern.

"Yes." Darcy admitted. "I told her I wanted her with me for the ashes ceremony." But Darcy's happy smile was gone, driven away by her worry for Jane. Her mother's anguished expression bothered Darcy almost as much as Jane's condition.

Bong, bong. Mary's phone signaled the arrival of a text message. "Hey Darcy, would you check that for me, please."

"Sure." Darcy glanced at the screen and her eyes widened with surprise. "It's from JoAnne." Darcy looked at her mother for any clues as to why JoAnne would be texting, now of all times, but saw nothing in her mother's eyes.

"Read it to me, please." Her mother said, sounding confident, but Darcy saw some doubt in her eyes. Her mother turned a corner and Darcy could see they were getting close to the water at Marina del Ray.

The message opened up and Darcy read it aloud. "I'm here, Mary. You sure about this?" How cryptic. Darcy looked at her mom, awaiting instructions.

"Text back. Say, 'Absolutely. Be there in five.'" Her Mom tried to smile but only managed a grimace before taking a deep ragged breath. Something was up. Darcy could feel her insides beginning to churn. First Jane and now her mother and this mysterious JoAnne person.

Darcy watched her mother as she turned into the marina parking lot. Suddenly, she seemed different, seemed anxious. She was usually so calm and collected. Even when Darcy's father had died, she had been in control. Something about this JoAnne person, the woman her mother was NOT having a sexual relationship with. *Jeez. Why did you have to say it that way, Mom?* And this woman was waiting for them and her father's ashes at the boat?

As her mom navigated the parking lot, Darcy looked back at Jane. Now, she looked sick, really sick; sweaty, pale, and shaking. Darcy reached over the seat for Jane's hand, ignoring her mother. It felt clammy, and there was no response to her touch. "Mom! Stop the car. Jane's sick! I need to get into the back seat." Her voice was shaking. "Please."

"I'm pulling in now. What do you mean?" She wheeled the car into the a parking space at the marina.

Darcy jumped out and yanked the back door

open. "Jane! Jane. What's the matter?" She did not whisper and she did not see her mom's tears begin. She lifted Jane into her arms and moved her over, totally unaware of how her actions appeared to her mother.

Jane's eyes fluttered open. "Can't stay ... too far. It's like I'm stretching, too thin. Damn, it hurts. Sorry Darcy." Her head flopped back and she disappeared.

"Jane!" Darcy cried out and flopped down into the back seat.

CHAPTER TEN

"Darcy!" She heard her mother's desperate, nearly panicked voice, beside her. "You tell me what's going on right now! You hear me. Right now!" She had come around to the passenger side rear door and was staring at her through tears as she leaned into the car.

Darcy looked up into her mother's tear streaked face and grabbed her around the neck, letting her own tears begin to fall. After a moment, Darcy slid over and Mary sat down in the back beside her. Darcy's mind worked overtime. What was she going to say. The truth? Some version of it? A complete fabrication? *Double damn! What am I going to do?*

"Already told you about Jane, the other day." Darcy hoped that it would do.

"We talked about hallucinations and imaginary people to talk to. What happened a few moments ago was different and down right frightening. I need the truth, Darcy." Her mother's words were strong but her expression was worried.

Darcy hung her head. Time for the whole truth. "Mom. There are times when I do see a girl, invisible to everyone but me. And yes, she's not imaginary, nor is she an hallucination. She is just invisible to everyone but me. I think she is a ghost, a spirit, somehow trapped here. She only appears to me. She is my age and we do talk a lot. I call her Jane because she doesn't know her real name. She remembers almost nothing from her life, and she has become my very best friend, ever. A few minutes ago, she looked real sick and just faded away ... gone. I was, I am, very worried about her."

"No, no, NO!" Her mother buried her face in her hands. "You are going to talk to that psychologist when we get back. You hear me? Today!"

"I know it sound's bad, Mom, but Jane is in trouble and I'm trying to help her get free from whatever is trapping her in this limbo." Darcy sighed. That didn't help her much, but it sounded true, felt true. Trapped in limbo, in between, not here, not there, not dead, not quiet alive, lost. *Damn. I have to help Jane.*

Her mother got out of the car and walked around to retrieve the urn with Darcy's father's ashes. She looked through the car at Darcy.

"Today!"

"Yes, Mom." Best not to argue or push back just now.

As Darcy trailed her mother down the long dock, Darcy wondered what Jane had meant by 'too far'. Too far from what? Her thoughts were interrupted by her mother's voice ahead of her. "Captain John. JoAnne. This is my daughter, Darcy Marie."

Darcy looked up from the wood planks of the dock to the captain, a darkly tanned middle aged man with windswept white hair and a relaxed demeanor. He smiled broadly and stuck out his hand. *Cool, a handshake.* She shook it. He seemed like a good, friendly man. Then she moved her view to JoAnne, the mystery woman; a nice looking, early to mid-thirties brunette, like her Darcy's mother, but with secrets haunting her dark circled eyes.

Darcy held out her hand like she had done for the Captain, but JoAnne brushed right by it and grabbed her in a full body hug, touching from head to toe. Darcy stiffened; too much contact, too close. She controlled her need to pull away for her mother's sake, but her arms still hung down by her sides, passively.

JoAnne hugged Darcy for what seemed like five minutes before she pushed her back by the shoulders and said, "I can't believe it. I finally get to meet the mysterious and much discussed Darcy."

Darcy forced a weak smile, knowing she should have returned the hug, but she wasn't used to being hugged by strangers, unless they were an invisible naked ghost. She smiled wide and warmly in her mind, picturing Jane.

"Nice to meet you too." Darcy said, formally, studying JoAnne who did seem to be struggling with something difficult. Her smile, though wide, did not lighten the dark shadows in her eyes.

"Get on board," the captain announced. "We have an hour out and an hour back. Don't want to be out after it gets dark, today."

They all boarded the private excursion boat and Darcy commandeered a bench at the stern in the sun and wind, finding it exhilarating and almost private. The wind formed a cocoon around her. From within the envelop of salty breeze, she watched her mother and JoAnne as they sat high up under the awning covering the flying bridge. They talked like old friends, smiling and laughing. They would pat each others legs and shoulders, or even hold hands, as they shared so many words, smiles, and maybe secrets. Darcy watched JoAnne come near tears several times and her mother comforting her. She could tell that they were close, real close.

How could her mother have a friend, that close, without her knowing, unless she specifically wasn't supposed to know. Then she remembered JoAnne saying, 'finally get to meet the mysterious and much discussed Darcy'. Finally? Much discussed? Her mom kissed JoAnne's cheek and Darcy nodded. Looks like her mom as a secret friend too, but of course, JoAnne wasn't invisible or naked.

Was Jane alright? She had disappeared before and come back fine. Or was she really sick ... or really gone this time? Darcy sighed. She had truly wished Jane could have been here with her for this, her final goodbye to her father. She had wanted to share her father's ceremony with Jane. Suddenly a smile graced her face as the solution dawned on her and she jumped up and wobbled forward into the cabin as the boat rocked a little on the waves. "Captain, Do you have a pen and some paper. I want to write a note to put into the urn before we give my father to the sea."

He grinned and led her down into the small cabin where he pointed to a small desk with everything she would need. She thanked him and quickly composed a note, expressing on paper, what she had not been able to say in person. She folded it before coming back topside.

Climbing up to her mother and JoAnne on the flying ridge, she pushed her hair from her face and smiled. "Mom, I wrote a note to Dad and I want to put in the urn before we give him to the ocean. Please."

"Is it private or can you read it to us?" The

question seemed straight forward. Her mother seemed much more relaxed now, sitting there beside her friend, JoAnne. Darcy smiled. Everyone needs a friend. That, she knew for sure. Darcy didn't feel that her mother was pressuring her for the note and she did want to share it, but she hesitated just a little as she glanced over at JoAnne. She was still just a touchy-feely stranger to Darcy.

Her mother reached out and gently grasped Darcy's hand. "If it's private between you and your father. I understand." Darcy saw the understanding in her mother's eyes and heard it in her voice. When she looked closer at JoAnne, she saw a soft warm and welcoming smile under her eyes that were dark and hollow, with depths of sorrow and loss.

Darcy needed to be truthful, for her father, for Jane, for everyone. Those ashes, sitting between her mother and JoAnne were going to be the last part of her father she would ever see. She desperately wanted him to know some things that she had not been able to say in life. She unfolded the note and read.

"Dad, for the first week after you left me, I hated you for leaving. I couldn't tell anyone and I kept it deep inside me, festering. That was the very selfish part of me. The better part of me, always knew, always understood your decision. I had seen you bravely and silently suffer all those years, trapped inside your own head. But all that time, I was too scared and too weak, to even come into your room and hug you. I would close my eyes and run by. I'm so sorry that I squandered those opportunities to show you my love. But a week ago, I found a friend, now my very best friend, who I call Jane. She has helped me through this very difficult time and I wanted you to know about her. She is funny, caring, and a little bit of a smart ass. You would have loved her as I do. I wanted her here with me as I say goodbye but she couldn't be here, she's sick. So please accept this note from me as a sign that I do love you. My friend Jane would have loved you too. Please know that I will be fine and I will help Mom. Goodbye Dad. Please rest peacefully on your travels."

She looked up at her mother and JoAnne, both of whom were weeping and holding each others hands. Her mother jumped up and wrapped Darcy in her arms till she had to struggle free. "Mom. I love you too, but got to breathe."

Her mother held out the urn and opened it while Darcy dropped in the folded note. Darcy noticed that JoAnne, quietly and almost unnoticed, had placed her hand reverently against the side of the urn. JoAnne was the mysterious one, not her.

"We're here. We're in the current." The captain announced and the three of them walked the urn to the stern of the boat. Darcy held the urn equally with her mother and JoAnne and poured the ashes of her father, and her former life, into the Pacific ocean. They all cried, including JoAnne. Darcy watched her through her own tears. JoAnne wasn't acting. She was truly grieving.

Who was she? If her mother had kept JoAnne a secret this long, Darcy guessed she would have to wait for her mother to explain. Pressing her would be inappropriate and insensitive, but her curiosity was severely piqued.

Mary and JoAnne said a teary goodbye at the marina, before Darcy and her mother rode home silently, the only sounds were deep breathing and road noise. Darcy worried about Jane all the way back to the house, thankful that her mother had not questioned her further about her. In return, she did not ask anything about JoAnne. As Darcy later stood on the small front porch waiting for her mother to open the door to the house, she hoped Jane would be asleep in the bed when she got upstairs.

Her mother took Darcy by her shoulders. "That was the most beautiful note you wrote and it showed me some real maturity, so I'm going to let this Jane thing slide a while, as she does seem to be helping you, somehow. But, sometime soon, you will have to resolve your, uh, Jane issue. You can't let something like that go on much longer, understand?"

"Thanks, Mom. I will ... uh ... Mom, now that

I've met her, I have to ask. Who is JoAnne, really?" She knew she probably should not have asked, but her curiosity won the day.

Her mom sighed and turned briefly to face the driveway before facing Darcy again. "I'll say just this much. She's a kind, loving, smart, and wonderful person, as I hope you saw this afternoon. I will explain more later, but right now, just know that she is suffering through a terrible personal crisis in her life and I am trying to help her. Please let that be enough details for now, okay?"

"Sure." Darcy hugged her mother. "I guess we both have secret friends."

Her mom frowned for a moment, then smiled thinly and kissed her cheek. Darcy ran into the house and ran upstairs, where she stopped, panting at the bedroom door. There was Jane, lying in bed, asleep and covered up to her neck. Darcy was so happy to see her that she ran and leaped onto the bed. "Jane. Thank the stars in the sky! Are you okay?"

Jane startled awake with a shriek. "What are you doing? Trying to frighten me to death, maybe again." She laughed then grimaced in pain, moaning and scrunching up into a fetal ball.

"Jane! What's wrong?"

"Stomach ... really hurts ..." Jane rolled back and forth in agony.

Darcy threw back the covers and pushed her

down onto the bed. Jane's abdomen had a bleeding, finger-sized hole in it, on her left side just under her ribs. Blood continued to ooze from it for a moment then it suddenly puckered and became perfectly round. Darcy stared at the wound. "You're hurt! What is that?"

"I don't know." Jane scowled in pain, fighting tears. "Damn! It hurts."

Darcy grabbed a handful of tissues but they would not touch Jane's skin. Since only her hand could touch Jane, she gently rubbed Jane's stomach all around the apparent injury, knowing that it was probably a useless gesture, but she was desperate to do something for her. Jane continued to grimace in pain, and after a few moments of gentle touching all around the injury, the hole faded and disappeared. "Thank the stars above. It's gone." She hugged Jane, pulling her close. "When you faded away in the car, I was so worried."

Darcy sat up and Jane followed suit. "Aren't you going to make a snide comment about my nakedness."

"I don't care, as long as your here." Darcy leaned down and squeezed her again.

"Even if I wiggle and writhe, like this?" She began to move around provocatively.

"Ah, Jeez. I'm going to go shower." Darcy bounced off the bed laughing. Smart ass, happy Jane was back. Darcy's world felt whole again and she felt happy. *No,* she thought. *Not just happy, I feel wonderful!*

She dropped her clothes in the hamper and climbed into the large shower and suddenly there was Jane leaning against the back wall. "Jane! I love you, but I'm still not all that comfortable being naked in front of other people, and you know it." But she didn't cover up or turn around.

"You love me? Why, I'm just a ghost, maybe even an hallucination. Remember." she just grinned with her arms crossed until Darcy sighed and turned around and began to soap up.

Darcy smiled broadly as she scrubbed, just happy that Jane was back. She continued to shower, not knowing if Jane was watching or had gone. But then she heard Jane behind her, "You know, I love you too ... prude."

"Trollop." Darcy parried. When she turned back around, after rinsing off, Jane had disappeared. Darcy really laughed the first time in weeks.

She turned off the water, dried, wrapped her hair in the towel, and left the bathroom walking toward her bedroom. Suddenly, she saw her mom walk up the stairs from the kitchen, and heading down the hall toward her own bedroom. She was wearing only her short nightie. "Hey, Mom, too hot in the house for clothes?"

Her mom laughed. "Well, Look at you. I, at least, have on a nightie. Be nice. Besides, its just you and me." She disappeared into her bedroom.

"Yeah! You, me, and Yahudi." She yelled after her mother. Then she heard Jane laughing from behind her.

"Here comes Yahudi." Jane said as she walked from the bathroom. She was naked as always but now looked dripping wet.

"How can you get wet? You're the strangest damn ghost I've ever known."

"Just how many ghosts have you known?"

"Shut up, you bare banshee." She laughed and sauntered to her room.

Jane was already there laying in bed when she got there. "Mighty big words for a cheerleader dropout wimp with nudity issues."

"Jane?" Darcy said as she slipped her nightgown on.

"What?"

"This may sound strange. I know you have something going on, maybe something serious or terrible for you that you have little control of. But, you being here with me, now, at this time in my life ... well, thanks. I really needed a friend ... even a naked one."

Jane laughed. "Happy to help. If I could control where and when I appeared, I would just stay here. There is something about you that draws me. I feel alive when I am near you. When I go away, it's like I cease to exist."

"Tomorrow, let's start finding out who you really are!"

"Thanks for saying are, and not was. Night Darcy."

"Sleep tight Jane."

CHAPTER ELEVEN

After sleeping late on Sunday, Darcy awoke and found Jane gone from the bed. She was often missing in the mornings and Darcy put her worry aside, at least temporarily. She found her mother lounging in the kitchen in her short robe and a cup of coffee. Darcy smiled gently to herself. She was not going to react in any way nor say a word.

"You'll have to fix your own breakfast this morning, kitchen staff is off duty on Sunday," her mother said, huddled over her cup across the table.

"Funny, Mom." Darcy fixed herself toast and coffee and sat down. Jane was still not there and Darcy hoped she was alright considering the stomach injury scare last night.

They sat quietly for a few minutes, each staring into their coffee, until Darcy's mother sighed deeply like she does when something needs to be said, something difficult or critical. Darcy's heart nearly skipped a beat. What now? More about Jane? More about JoAnne?

"Sweetie, I have invited JoAnne over for lunch today, okay?" She finished the last swallow of her coffee. "It's time for us to start being less mysterious in this family. Right?" Darcy saw pleading in her mother's eyes.

Did her mother want privacy? Was she in the way, somehow? "Uh, no problem Mom. I can find something to do. I have some research and I need to study for ..."

"No, Dear. I meant lunch with the both of us. I need you here. There are things we need to discuss. Things you need to know. JoAnne is going to be in our lives even more, soon." Her mother set her cup in the dish washer but didn't turn around. She just leaned on the counter almost like she was in pain.

Now, Darcy was worried. "Sure, just holler. I'll be upstairs on the my laptop." Where was Jane? Now she needed Jane more than ever ... more JoAnne. What did that mean?

Her mother turned around and caught Darcy's eye. "Change of topic ... did Jane come back last night?" Her mom's expression was guarded.

Darcy studied her mother's expression for a few moments before answering. Her mom would never be intentionally cruel, but she did look like it was a serious question. Darcy kept her voice level and her manner respectful. "Mom, you don't really believe that Jane is real. Why ask?"

Her mom's face fell and she sat back down. "I'm in new territory here and kinda lost. My life has been bound up in secrets and dark shadows. I'm trying to be more transparent and you'll have to help me. I am just trying to participate in your life. Jane may not be real for me, but she is obviously real for you." She reached across the table and took Darcy's hand. "I just want to be a bigger, open part of your life. I want to help. I want you to know that I'm here for you."

Darcy looked at her mother's hand on hers and a weight lifted from her shoulders. Her mother was willing to work with her about Jane and she got up and ran around to her, hugging her in her chair. "Thank you. And yes, she appeared last night but only for a short while, then disappeared again. She had some kind of stomach injury. And she's still not here, this morning. I'm worried, again, almost like yesterday."

Darcy backed up a little, happy with her mother's support but still feeling that something was amiss. Something was still about to happen and her mother was still visibly tense. "Mom? What's going on, really? This isn't just about Jane is it? There's more. Right?"

"Yes, for the last sixteen years, and in reality, beginning much earlier, this family has become a house of secrecy … a collection of secrets, of separate paths, and of silence. I'm sure your father would not have wanted that. In fact, I know he didn't. It was the one topic we ever really argued about. As you have grown older, you have been demanding more information about your father's history and mine as well. So, I'm going to start being more open with you about your dad's and my family and our family ... but, I want you to be open about your life as well. Real or not real, I don't want you to bear your burdens alone as I begin to share mine. Secrets become heavier, the older they are. Eventually, they break you and cripple your ability to be happy. I know this from painful experience. Time to stop the secrets, all of us."

"Wow, Mom. You sound like a psychologist."

Mary grinned. "I didn't drag you with me but I did go see that doctor I mentioned to you earlier, Dr. Alice Norman. She said she would be glad to speak to you, but really what we needed to do was to throw the old rotting secrets out into the light to dry up and blow away. We need to be honest with each other."

"I like her," Darcy said. "I'm with you all the way on this." Darcy leaned over and hugged her Mom again. "I'll be ready for lunch."

She almost ran up the steps to her room. Things were going to change and her world became several shades lighter. Even homework seemed more agreeable. As she studied, working on her English paper about Norse Mythology, a favorite topic, she kept looking over her shoulder at the bed where Jane often appeared. Even as she wrote about the implications, in today's society, of the metaphor of Thor's hammer, she worried about Jane. The paper grew in length and footnoted content but at a sluggish pace. She just could not concentrate, with her worries about Jane being every other thought.

When the doorbell finally rang just before noon, Jane was still missing, and Darcy gave up on the paper. She walked downstairs to lunch with her mom and JoAnne, unsure of what to expect in conversation. But she liked her mother's purpose for the gathering.

"Darcy!" JoAnne said, as she hugged her like a long lost friend, again. Darcy recognized that JoAnne was one of those touchy-feely people who hugs you, holds your arms or shoulders, pats your cheeks, and runs their fingers through your hair, all while talking to you, recognizing no personal space at all. Darcy accepted it because she was her mom's friend and because she actually felt less put off by the contact, but it still took some effort. JoAnne ran her hand down Darcy's hair and her eyes filled with tears before she turned away and hugged Mary with a sob. Darcy froze. That was weird.

Her mom had prepared a giant Italian salad and homemade bread sticks. While they ate, Darcy noticed that the conversations covered only generic topics of general interest, nothing at all even tangentially related to why JoAnne was her mom's friend. Darcy grunted a few times, anxious to get to the important stuff, but no luck until her mother finally stood up.

"Let's go sit into the living room. We have a lot to talk about." Mary looked at Darcy and smiled. "Finally, right?" Darcy smiled. Her mother really knew her too well.

JoAnne spun around and reached into the huge shopping bag she called a purse. "I have a wonderful light red wine I want to share. Mary, I assume that Darcy doesn't do wine yet."

Mary looked at Darcy. "No, she doesn't. Sorry Darcy, but you're not old enough yet."

"No problems, Mom. I'll just get a beer," Darcy said straight faced as she got up and headed toward the refrigerator.

"You'll get a what?" Her Mother asked from under lowered brows, her voice a little shocked, but JoAnne chuckled like she had understood Darcy's sarcasm and winked at her.

"A soda, mom. I said I'll have a soda." Darcy grinned as she reached into the fridge.

JoAnne laughed and grabbed Mary's arm. "That's just like I remember someone else, back when, a true smart ass."

"I remember it the other way round," Mary

said, laughing too, as she sat down on the sofa.

Darcy sat beside her mother and JoAnne sat in the large chair before she took a long sip of her wine. "Mary, may I start this difficult conversation?"

"Sure, I already told Darcy that we all needed to start being more transparent, that this family has too long been wrapped up in deep secrets." Her mother reached over and patted Darcy's knee

Darcy was getting more nervous by the second. *Deep secrets, wow.*

"Darcy," Joanne began. "Your mother is right. It is past time to begin to expose the enigma that is your family, both its darkness and its pain."

Darkness and pain? Darcy sat wide eyed. What an intro. She was already barely hanging in at school and at home. She had a ghost for a best and only friend, and no extended family. What more darkness and pain could she handle? She heard JoAnne call her name through the fog of her worry.

"Darcy. I can see from your expression that you are apprehensive about this. Don't be, just listen. You need to hear this ... and your mother and I need to say it out loud." JoAnne scooted to the front of her chair. "I am going to start by telling you the story of your mom and I. But, I'll start in the middle, with your mother's marriage to your dad."

Darcy thought quickly. *They knew each other way back then? Wow.*

JoAnne continued. "I was the maid of honor at their wedding and I was working for your father back then in the early days of his company. Later, when you were still in there," she pointed to her Mary's belly. "Your father took me, his managerial assistant, on a business trip to Seattle and ..."

"It was you?" Darcy's eye widened as she realized where JoAnne was going with her story. "Dad had an affair with you?"

"Yes. Not my best behavior or judgment, but I loved him and I always had, even back as far as college. You know, we three were at college together and your mother and I both fell for him there."

"No, I didn't know." Darcy said. "I didn't know about the affair until last week. And I didn't know about you at all until a few days ago."

Her mom nodded and interrupted. "I told you how he came home after that trip, quilt ridden, and how I forgave him. What I did not tell you was that for the next thirteen years, JoAnne and I, for your dad's sake, remained in contact with each other, but we were just barely civil. We nearly hated each other over your dad."

JoAnne reached out and grabbed Darcy's arm. Darcy resisted the impulse to pull away. "We finally resolved most of our issues and have been much closer from about the time Gary ... your father, became bedridden."

Darcy frowned at her mother. "All those years, angry. What a waste. Mom. I can see why you'd be mad at ... uh, Miss JoAnne, but not the other way around."

JoAnne nodded. "No one is innocent in any of this, not even your dad. While we were together, Gary continually assured me he would leave your mom and would be with me forever. I blamed Mary for forcing him to stay with her, and for stealing him away from me."

Darcy sucked in her breath to begin another set of questions but her mother started first. "Before you get too wound up, Darcy. You must realize that your father was at fault here as much as JoAnne for the affair itself, but all the anger and pain and suffering that followed ... that was the fault of all three of us. We made a cascade of serious mistakes and it took nearly sixteen years to come to grips with it, for all three of us." She leaned forward toward Darcy. "But, by any measure, JoAnne and I are mostly to blame for the years of relationship hell we put ourselves and our families through because we were not mature enough to see the damage we were doing as we nursed our hurt."

JoAnne took Mary's hand in both of hers, before looking at Darcy again. "We let our passion for your father tear us apart. Your mom is a wonderful person and always has been. I don't know why I took so long to rediscover that fact. Love you

Mary."

"Darcy," her mother said and waited until Darcy looked her in the eyes. "JoAnne is a beautiful, giving person and I am also sorry it took me all those years to remember it. I'd known her since she was born. We had played together and lived together till I went away to college."

Darcy frowned, putting two and two together. "Wait. What is your last name Miss JoAnne?"

"Baker. And please stop calling me miss. I'm only thirty-six."

"Mom! That's the same as your maiden name. Your guys are sisters!"

CHAPTER TWELVE

Darcy grinned. Her world had just gotten bigger, finally. She had an aunt, Aunt JoAnne. She looked at her mom and her aunt. Maybe now she would hear even more about her mom's side of the family.

"Yes." Her mother said, smiling at JoAnne. "The very same family name. Sisters, and we both loved the same man, your father. He and JoAnne had that brief period of weakness and I, in my rage, caused me and my sister to loose years of our lives to that anger and resentment and it tore our family apart. What a waste."

"I thought you said you stayed in contact," Darcy said, frowning. "Why, when you were so mad at each other?"

Mary grasped Darcy's hand. "Mad doesn't quiet cover it, but yes, we stayed in contact ... your father wished it, demanded it actually and there were other reasons too. There is more to this story but I feel that this was a good start and probably enough for today."

"Mom! Don't leave me hanging." Darcy said moving to the edge of her seat. "I've spent my entire life without any extended family. This is great! Don't stop now."

Darcy's mother got up and paced a few times back and forth in front of the sofa before returning resuming her seat. "JoAnne?"

Darcy watched JoAnne's face flash through several emotions. "Only the past ... not ready yet for the future."

"Okay." Mary said as she placed her hand on JoAnne's shoulder. "When Gary was diagnosed with Muscular Dystrophy and we realized how it must end, even with the best of medical care, the three of us made our peace with fate, and JoAnne and I began to fix the issues between us. Without her, I would never have made it through your father's decline and death."

JoAnne closed her eyes for a moment, then looked straight at Darcy. "When your father returned home, after our affair, he honored his commitment to your mother and to you, as he should have, as husband and ... father. But I still loved him and did till the day he died. I also grieved with his illness and death. Mary understood that and supported me through his illness and death as well."

Darcy grinned and offered a rare hug to her aunt which was greedily accepted. "Aunt JoAnne. Nice to meet you!"

Having an aunt was great but she frowned and looked at her mother. Maybe she could push the opening a little wider. "What about grandparents, your parents? Before, you would never talk about them, even when I asked you point blank. I have always been one of the few kids who had no grandparents, no aunts, no uncles, not even cousins. Are you going to tell me about your parents now? Please."

Mary got up. "You are absolutely right. Let's all take a ride. Time to catch up on some history, and expand your family a little further."

They left the house and all three of them got into Mary's car, Darcy in the back seat, silently mystified. No one spoke for at least ten minutes until JoAnne sighed and looked back over the seat at Darcy and grimaced. "Mary, you sure this is the best way to introduce this topic?"

Mary nodded. "We need the visual to explain."

Darcy felt confused. What were they talking about? All she had asked about was grandparents? A visual? "Mom, you're being mysterious again."

"Yes, I know, but you will understand better when you see ... it."

Darcy began to wonder if they were going to a

cemetery but she kept her thoughts private. They drove for almost an hour in the Sunday afternoon traffic before Darcy recognized where they were. "Wow, mom. We're in Brentwood. Look at those houses!"

"Yes. But actually, we're going through Brentwood, to just outside the city limits." Her mother said without further explanation.

Had to be a cemetery. Darcy was almost sure until the car finally stopped alongside a high white fence surrounding several hundred acres of green pastures with small groves of shade trees and grazing horses. Just up ahead, where the white rail fence turned into a brick wall, Darcy saw a large wrought iron gate. In iron scrollwork letters, it read, The Baker Estate.

"Darcy, pay close attention, now," her mother said, still being cryptic. Her suggestion about attending was unnecessary. Darcy was enthralled with the view and the intrigue.

Mary drove ahead and entered a code at the gate before driving along the long curving driveway. After cruising at least a quarter of a mile, she followed the driveway as it curved into a large circle surrounding a giant fountain with leaping stone dolphins shooting sprays of water. She drove under the great porte cochere and pulled back around to the far side of the fountain before stopping the car.

Darcy stared through the car window at a large, multistory, multiple winged, stone mansion with that astounding porte cochere, covering both lanes of the large circular driveway. Her attention was drawn immediately to the left wing of the mansion. A skeleton of blackened stone was all that remained of its one time magnificence.

Darcy slid over even closer to the window and lowered it, ogling the mansion. The center section and the other wings seemed to be intact. Darcy noticed that the two intact wings even looked lived in. "What in the world happened to that part? And it looks like someone is living in the other parts." She looked at her mother and then Aunt JoAnne.

Darcy's mother was calm and expressionless but Aunt JoAnne was sitting with her hand over her mouth, stifling sobs. Mary spoke in a hushed voice, her hand laying on JoAnne's shoulder. "JoAnne and I lived here in this wonderful place with our wonderful parents until a supposedly accidental fire killed them and our carefree life of childhood. I was thirteen and she was twelve."

"Supposedly?" Darcy frowned. "You think it was set on purpose?"

Aunt JoAnne was still crying too hard to answer and Darcy's mother sighed as she often did when having to speak about something distasteful. "Nothing was ever proved, but JoAnne and I feel sure it was a certain relative who thought she would inherit it all, or a large portion of the estate. She didn't know that the will had already been secretly changed."

"Who was this relative? We're being painfully truthful now, right?" Darcy said.

Mary looked at JoAnne who nodded her acquiescence. "JoAnne and I have an older sister, Hanna, and that gives you have another aunt. But she was then and still is a terrible person who was always in trouble with the law." Mary shrugged and frowned.

"How long did you live there after that?"

"We had to move out." Mary said sadly. "The Estate went into probate until the will could be attested and all questions answered. Relatives came out of the woodwork like roaches after a crumb. The courts were filled with petitions and fillings for years. Even Hanna battled for it."

JoAnne took a deep breath. "Thank goodness, after our parents deaths, we were sent to live with some much poorer relatives instead of Hanna. She's in jail right now for a robbery where someone got killed, a life sentence. She was never charged with the Baker fire."

Mary looked up. "What a horrible, sordid family we have. After the fire, Hanna, our older sister, tried to adopt us and sued the courts for custody, but a more distant relative of our Mother also fought for us in court. It was a terrible time.

They both wanted us because they thought we would inherit the estate. And as bad as they turned out to be, we're still glad the older couple got us instead of our sister."

"Were they mean?" Darcy tried not to imagine her mother or JoAnne in such circumstances. "Were you abused?"

"I think they resented us for not receiving a bigger slice of the estate for caring for us." JoAnne swallowed, barely controlling her tears. "They didn't beat us or anything. They ignored us, almost felt worse. They were cold and uncaring, like we didn't exist. We knew we had a house over our heads only as long as they got their monthly allotment check. We got out as soon as we could, first Mary, then me, a year later. We both went to college at Stanford University."

Mary shrugged. "The estate was caught up in court battles until after we had graduated from college. It took that long for the will to be validated and all issues resolved."

Suddenly Darcy felt Jane's presence and jerked her eyes sideways but all she saw was the last of Jane's form already fading from sight. She looked almost as sick as she had at Marina Del Ray; too far again?

Mary looked over the back seat at Darcy, oblivious of Jane's brief appearance. "We both met your father at the same college party and he was so real, so full of caring, we both fell for him. We actively competed for him for almost two years."

Darcy could understand that, but it was still hard to see her father as a man with a serious weakness in his ability to honor commitment. Time to think about something else. "Who owns that mansion now? Who's living there now." Darcy pointed to the intact part of the building.

"The estate care takers and house servants live there still. But, actually ..."

JoAnne grabbed Mary's arm, frowning, with the barest negative shake of her head. "No."

"You own it." Mary finished her announcement.

"What?"

"It is being held in trust for you and any other grandchildren that ..." Mary stopped and looked at JoAnne. "That may arise."

"For me? When I'm, like eighteen or something?" Darcy stared at the monster building. "Wait. I have cousins? There are other grandchildren?"

JoAnne stifled a sob and stepped quickly out of the car. Darcy watched her walk unsteadily around to the driver's side front finder where she leaned back on the car, crying and gazing at her old house.

"Mom, is she okay?"

"She was here when the fire that killed our parents started. I was away at a party. She got out, but had to stand here in the yard, almost where we are right now, as the house burned and our parents died."

Darcy gulped a couple of deep breaths to keep her own sympathetic tears under control and got out of the car. She walked up beside Aunt JoAnne, placing her arm around her back. "I'm so sorry. Mom told me about your parents. You okay?"

JoAnne looked up into Darcy's face and ran her hand through Darcy's hair and began shaking with gut wrenching sobs. She slumped sideways against Darcy. "I miss her so much. God help me!"

Darcy held her and looked over into the car at her mom, pleading for help with her eyes. Mary jumped out and supported JoAnne's other side. "Come on. Let's get back in. Time to go."

By the time JoAnne was seated, she had calmed greatly and she reached into the back seat for Darcy's hand. "Thank you sweetie ... when you're eighteen, you'll get a partially burned out building but there were a lot of great memories there too. They were only bad at the end." She squeezed Darcy's hand and looked at Mary, tears glistening in her eyes. "Her hand is so warm, so like ..."

Without warning, Jane appeared beside Darcy again, looking sick and weak. Her skin was glistening with sweat and her eyes pleading for help. They pulled at Darcy's heart. But, like before, she faded quickly and was gone, looking very much like she did at the marina.

Mary interrupted JoAnne, equally unaware that Jane had made a brief appearance, and continued the conversation. "Both JoAnne and I still get a monthly allotment from the estate which helps with expenses."

Darcy sat up straight. "Wait! With that money coming in, you probably don't have to work at all, do you?"

"True. But I never could just stay home, even before your father got ill. JoAnne still works for your father's company. She's the new local branch manager." Mary patted JoAnne's hand. "She was always the smart one with computers like your Dad."

"What about all that medical equipment and nursing care, his company's medical insurance, right?" Darcy had always wondered about that.

"Yes. Dad's company and insurance paid for most of the medical stuff and the nursing care. The Baker Estate also paid a small monthly amount for his support as my husband. I worked for my own mental health, especially toward the end." Her mom sighed again.

"What about Dad's parents?" Darcy decided to ask, though she had never gotten an answer before to this same question. "You did say you wanted to be more open, right?"

Mary looked at JoAnne who shrugged, before

she answered. "His father had disowned him when he was eighteen because he entered Stanford University to study computers and math and other ungodly subjects." She paused for a few moments. Darcy could tell that she was still angry with his family, even now, twenty years later. "Your father had always been expected to become a minister in their church, following in the footsteps of his father. However, when he turned eighteen he legally changed his last name from Johnson to Winters and escaped his family."

Darcy sat back in the seat. Her last name was not a name with a long history, it was made up. "Winters ... then, there is no family line behind that name?"

"No. Your father's bloodline is in the Johnson family line from the Boulder City, Nevada area."

JoAnne looked into the back seat. "But the freedom he achieved from changing his name, also cost him his entire extended family; his local community, and a much younger sister. The next time your dad had contact was in 2003 after his father had become ill. Your dad felt the need to visit his father one last time. And ... well, the visit went badly, very badly. He was forced to leave and never returned again."

"A younger sister?" Darcy said. "Then, I have another aunt?" Her mother and aunt both looked away and neither acknowledged her question. The conversation just stopped.

"Damn, that's cold." Jane suddenly said from beside Darcy, this time solid and much less sickly looking.

"Damn, Jane, where you been? And what happened those other two times. You just slipped away, zip, zap." Darcy said before she realized that Aunt JoAnne was in the car. "Sorry Aunt JoAnne, sometimes I like to pretend I have an imaginary friend."

"Darcy? Aunt JoAnne will be staying with us for a while as we move to resolve the issue she's dealing with. So, lets be truthful with Aunt JoAnne now, too. Okay?" Her mother said as JoAnne looked at Darcy with a quizzical expression.

Darcy looked at Jane, asking with her eyes if being truthful was okay with her. Jane shrugged her acceptance. "Jane is my best friend, but she is invisible to everyone but me. I think she is a trapped spirit and I'm really torn about helping her get to where she needs to be because that would mean I would loose her."

Jane smiled, looking at JoAnne. "Don't know about the other times. All I remember is feeling stretched like at the marina the other day. Who is this JoAnne person? Looks familiar. Actually, looks like your mom quite a bit."

"That's because she is my mother's younger sister. I never knew it, till today. This is my Aunt

JoAnne."

Darcy and Jane talked of driving for the upcoming test and her going out for soccer the following week as they rode back home. She didn't see her mother look at JoAnne with desperation or the tears that threatened to fall as she carried on her conversation with Jane. JoAnne squeezed Mary's shoulder in support.

CHAPTER THIRTEEN

When the alarm clock's peace killing buzzer went off Monday morning, Darcy rolled over to find Jane still asleep. "Time to get up, you sleepy head."

Jane slowly opened her eyes but she looked sick and groaned. "You know, if I wasn't a ghost, I'd smash that damn clock and beg to stay home from school today. I really don't feel good."

Darcy felt her forehead. It was hot. How can a ghost have a fever? "You've got a temp! No school for you today. Go back to sleep, my darling."

"Yes Mommy." Jane tried to laugh but coughed instead and rolled over to her other side and was asleep almost instantly. Darcy watched her laying in bed while she got herself ready for school but worrying about Jane threw her way off schedule. As she checked off the tasks she needed to get done before school, she lost track of time. The next thing she knew, she heard her mother's footsteps coming up the stairs and glanced at the clock. She was running late. It was way past time to head downstairs for breakfast. She walked to the bedside for one last look at Jane before her mother came in.

Just as Darcy reached the bedside, Jane faded away and the blanket settled onto the bed. Darcy hung her head. "Damn, gone again."

"Who's gone?" Her mother said as she entered the room.

"Jane." Darcy pointed at the blankets where Jane at been laying. The sheet and comforter now lay rumpled as if someone had recently been snuggling under them. Her mother frowned. "Looks like someone was in your bed."

"Yeah, Jane. She is feeling really bad this morning and will not be following me to school today." Darcy sighed and quickly straightened up her bed.

Mary walked to the bedside behind Darcy and hugged her. "Thank you for staying open with me about your ... friend Jane. We both must remain willing to talk as we work through this ghost thing." She ran one hand over the bedding. "That sure looked real, with the blanket like that." She released Darcy. "Come on. You're going to be late for school, again."

Darcy hung her head. Her mother was trying,

but obviously, she still did not really believe that Jane was real. What could she do? No one believed her. But Jane was real, she knew it in her heart and soul.

Half-way through first period, Darcy heard her name called out. "Darcy Winters, please report to the guidance counselor's office." She hung her head when she saw the other students grin at her. She knew they also heard what was implied but unsaid by that summons. "For a counseling session about Miss Winter's earlier and oh so public mental breakdown about naked people."

Ms. Carlyle smiled broadly as Darcy walked into the office. "Hi Darcy. How are you doing? It's been a few days since we talked last. How's it going?"

Darcy knew that Ms. Carlyle was trying to do a good thing but she felt so exposed when talking about private stuff. And it was her secrets-filled family to blame. Well, at least partially, any way. "Every time you call me out of class like that, the other kids all laugh and call me crazy under their breath. Can't we have a code or something, so everybody don't know where I'm going?" Darcy looked serious. She was serious.

"That's reasonable. I'll try to work out something. Tell me about your life now."

"Wow, that's broad." Darcy didn't know where to start, then she pictured her to-do list. "Let's see."

She talked about her love of cheer leading and her desire to be promoted back off the alternate list. The fact that her problems with Maisie, the team captain, was making that hard to do, was also mentioned. Joining the soccer team was also a desire of hers and she told the counselor that she was on the schedule to try out later in the week. Almost as an afterthought, she mentioned that she was getting much better grades.

Jane suddenly appeared in the chair beside her and she jumped, stifling a small startled squeal. Though Darcy downplayed her reaction, Ms. Carlyle noticed her sudden attention to the chair and frowned. "Let's talk about your invisible friend."

"I don't pretend that anymore. I'm done with that." Darcy felt terrible about lying with Jane sitting right there and Jane remained uncharacteristically quiet and still. Darcy hoped she had not insulted her.

"I hope so, Miss Winters. We'll talk again next week." She rose from her chair and opened her door. "You can go."

The hallway was empty as Darcy left the councilor's office and she immediately turned to Jane. "I'm so sorry. From your silence, I think I must have insulted you, but I had to say that, to keep her off my back."

Jane grinned, thinly. "I wasn't bothered by that. I understood. I'm just feeling like death warmed over. No pun intended."

"Why'd you appear here, then? Why not back at home? Don't you need the rest?"

"Yeah, I do, but I hate the gray void I'm in when I'm not with you. It don't feel real restful. And apparently, though I can appear in a different room from you, when you're there, school and your house is too far apart."

Darcy grimaced at the image of floating in a giant nothing. "I'm worried about you. We got to find out what's happening. In last period study hall, lets dig into more and better searches. Okay?" Darcy took her hand and began walking to the next class. Jane accompanied Darcy to each of her next several classes, staying with her through lunch. But as time passed, she looked sicker and weaker. By lunch time, she could barely keep her eyes open.

Jane laid her head on the lunch table just before Darcy finished eating and very slowly disappeared without even lifting her head. Darcy sighed. Her friend was suffering and she couldn't help. She managed to get through the afternoon classes without incident and almost ran into the library for her study hall, ready to do searches.

First, she searched for deaths of female teenagers with red hair within the last three months in California. There were several cases reported, but none of the girls were described as looking enough like Jane. Darcy expanded her parameters to include the entire west coast which increased the results by four cases. Even with the larger sample, the descriptions of the girls didn't provide any smoking guns in the search results.

Jane did not reappear until Darcy was ready for bed that night. She briefly appeared in bed and opened her eyes, but was so tired she fell back asleep before Darcy could discuss her latest search results with her. A few minutes later she slowly faded away, only to reappear in the wee hours of the morning, still asleep. Darcy couldn't return to sleep, worried that Jane would fade away again, and sat up watching her until time to get ready for school.

As Darcy was finishing getting dressed, Jane opened her eyes and grinned from the bed. "See ya at breakfast." Then she faded away just as Darcy left her room, heading for breakfast, herself.

When Darcy arrived at the table for breakfast, Jane was sitting at in her usual place. She was wearing a scarf and soft cap but nothing else. Darcy shook her head and sat down. "Nice scarf. Where's the rest of your outfit? That scarf just doesn't cover enough."

Jane ignored the rhetorical question and comment. "Did you see what I just did? I just relocated on purpose, in the real world, without going back to the void in between. Wow."

Darcy needed to discuss something that she had remembered while she was watching Jane sleep but first she reached to feel Jane's forehead. "Jane, should you be out of bed?" Well, you do look a little better. You sure you are okay enough to be up?"

"Yes. Thank you, Mommy." Jane glared at Darcy. "Did you hear what I just said about my accomplishment?"

"Oh, don't be such a smart ass. I couldn't sleep last night worrying about you." She shook her head as she saw Jane smirk. "What did you mean the other day when you were disappearing from the car. You said 'gone too far'. And the other day at the mansion you said you felt 'stretched'."

"I remember. It was really just a feeling, like I was being pulled back somewhere at the end of a giant rubber band." She coughed and held her stomach, suddenly looking thin and undernourished.

Darcy stood up and stared at her. "Look at you, your starving." But suddenly she was okay again and the scarf and hat was gone. Something wasn't right. "Maybe after I can drive, we can test your limits of distance and create some sort of map ... a stretch map."

"Yeah, let's do that." Jane said. "Then, maybe at the center of the stretch will be me ... my body. Man, I don't like the sound of that." She laid her head on the table and faded away again.

"Gone again," Darcy said and heard the sound of coffee being sipped across the table. *Damn!*

Forgot about Mom and Aunt JoAnne. They were at the table. How could she have missed that? She glanced over at them. Her mom had wanted her to be free and open about Jane and now she and JoAnne had both witnessed Darcy's side of a whole conversation. Neither had shown any reaction, or maybe had just successfully suppressed their reactions.

Nonetheless, Darcy felt she needed to explain. "Jane is not well, she's weak, like she's sick. She used to disappear and appear, poof, but now she just fades away or oozes into sight, well into my sight, anyway."

They both nodded noncommittally and continued eating until Darcy shook her head and left for school. She attended classes with misgivings and Jane failed to appear at school until Darcy's last period study hall in the library. Jane slowly became visible at the table with her head on her arms in the same position as the first time Darcy had interacted with her.

"Jane! Thank Goodness." Darcy managed to whisper loudly instead of shouting. "Are you okay?"

"Feeling weak but not too bad. What parameters were you going to use this time?"

"Well, frankly, I was going to spend a few minutes looking into my father's family. Mom won't even talk them and I'm curious. My school has an account at Ancestor dot com for History class. I am going to use it for my dad's family. Then I was going to look for you some more, but I already looked for female teenager deaths with your appearance with no real hits." She brought up the website.

"Sounds like fun. I'll help." Jane grinned but did not move.

They started with her father's name before he had changed it, Gary Abraham Johnson, but they found no matches, not even a record of his death. Darcy was dumbfounded. Then they looked at the specifically at the California death records and found him, but not with the name she knew him as. On the official record of Darcy's father's death, he was listed as Uriah Abraham Johnson, not Gary.

She risked a quick call to her mother at work. "Mom, I looked up Dads death record and it said his name was Uriah, not Gary. Is that true?"

Jane leaned in close with her ear near Darcy's and they both heard the response. "Yes. Your father had always hated his given name. He used Gary as a nickname when he entered college. Everyone had called him Gary there, even before I knew him. In fact, I didn't even know his real name until years after we were married."

After thanking her mother, they continued to dig into her father's family tree. They discovered that both his parents, Darcy's paternal grandparents, had died of natural causes in Boulder City, Nevada; his Mom in 1991, and his Dad in 2006. Darcy frowned. "I was already four years old before my grandfather died and they never, not once, even mentioned his name to me."

Darcy's father had been born in 1980, and his two older brothers, in 1972 and 1973. Both of his brothers had died in 1991 during the Persian Gulf War. They had been unmarried and had no children on record. Her father had a sister, Penelope, younger than he by ten years, born in October of 1990.

Darcy stopped writing her notes and scowled. "Mom told me that Dad had left home and changed his name when he was eighteen as he entered college. That would have been in 1998. His mother and brothers were all long dead by then and his little sister would only have been eight."

Jane lifted her head for a moment. "That means, it would have only been his father and sister and him at home. I wonder what was he escaping from." Jane asked as she laid her head back down on her arms that stretched across the table.

"Couldn't have been a little eight year old sister. My grandfather must have been hell on wheels," Darcy mused as she continued to search the family tree. She didn't bother with previous generations. She was interested in live relations, but she found no additional records. Apparently, her

Aunt Penelope was the only living relative from her fathers family and there was nothing about her on Ancestry dot com.

"That younger sister is all that's left of your father's line except for you. And it looks like she just disappeared off the face of the Earth." Jane didn't lift her head to speak. "Try Google. Maybe there is something about her from schools, newspaper articles, and such."

"Good idea." Darcy left the ancestry site and searched for any general internet hits on her father's sister's name, Penelope Johnson. She used the time period 1998 to 2006, during which she would have been at home with her father and in school. Darcy only found two search results, her birth announcement in a Boulder City newspaper, and a second newspaper article about a missing young teen called Penelope Johnson in 2004.

After broadening the time frame for her search, Darcy found another birth announcement, this one in a church bulletin. But it listed Penelope Johnson of Boulder City listed as the mother of a Tabitha Johnson born in 2004, in Missouri. "Hey, Jane, look. This has got to be her, even if it was in Missouri. How many Penelope Johnsons, born in 1990 in Boulder City, could there be? My Aunt Penelope had a daughter, Tabitha, born in 2004 in Hermann, Missouri. And Tabitha's only two years younger than me."

"Wow, you have a young cousin. What was she doing in Missouri?" Jane laid her head back down, beginning to fade. "So tired. I'm going. Bye."

There was no further information to be found and Darcy left school a few minutes early, hurrying home with her information about her father's family. Her mother was already home making a cup of coffee and Darcy plopped down at the table. "Home early today, good. Know what I did today?"

"What?"

"After you straightened out Dad's name for me, I researched him on Ancestor dot com and guess what? I found his sister, the one you mentioned so briefly the other day ... named Penelope who now has a daughter named Tabitha. That means I have both a young cousin and another aunt, but with the name Johnson, same name as Dad's real last name."

"You did what!" Her mother spun around toward her. "And yes! I am very well aware of that bitch!" She spun back around with her back to Darcy whose mouth fell open. She had never heard her mother speak so crudely before.

Her mom kept her back to Darcy for a long moment before heaving one of her deep sighs. "I was hoping to discuss your father's sordid family history with you when you were older, when you were at least eighteen, maybe even older ... or preferably, never."

"Eighteen? Never? Mom, what's going on?"

Darcy was still in shock over her mother's reaction. What was happening with her family? First her Mother and JoAnne hated each other for years. Now her Mother hates her young sister-in-law.

Her mother walked away into the living room and sat down on the sofa, suddenly changing subjects. "How are you and Jane doing?"

Darcy followed her and sat beside her. "You still want me to be completely honest with you about Jane, right?"

"Yes, of course."

"Well, at school and in other public places, I do not ... try not to, look at her, or talk to her. But I still see her and we are still best friends. But she is not doing real well. Seems, as time goes on, she's getting sicker and sicker." She closed her eyes and heaved a deep breath. "I lost Dad, watching him fade away until he died." Tears began to leak from between her closed eyelids. "Now, I think I'm watching Jane do the same."

Her mother extended her arms and Darcy accepted her embrace, crying on her shoulder. Mary spoke softly to her. "I'm so sorry sweetie. I wish I could help you."

"She is getting weaker and weaker. She stays gone longer and longer, and seems to be in pain more and more. I have to find a way to help her."

"What have you tried to do?"

Darcy sighed and sat back up. "She and I have

searched the internet together, and me alone, sometimes. We looked for teenage deaths with her appearance. We mostly just searched for recent deaths because she knows things from only a few months ago."

"Her appearance? What does she look like? You have never mentioned what she looks like."

Darcy's eyes widened. She had not even thought about that. No one but her knew what Jane looked like. "Well, she's my height and size, with the same red hair and green eyes ... looks like me a lot, actually. She even got her boobs early like me. But she isn't so bothered about nudity like me ... like I used to be anyway ... or maybe she just has no choice. She's always naked. I said that before, right?"

"No. You failed to mention that little piece of information. So, she looks like a naked you." Darcy's mother grinned a little. "That must have been torture for you, with your, uh, reaction to nudity."

"It was hard at first, but I'm kind of used to it now." Darcy paused. She hadn't really thought about how much they looked alike. But they really did. "After I get my license, we planned to test the issue of being 'too far' from something by creating a map. I think you heard part of that conversation. I assume, the thing in the center of that map will be her body. We want to drive in a bunch of directions and record her reactions to direction and distance. Then we could go to the real her ... her body."

Mary nodded in approval. "Also, people are sick and dying in hospitals. They are dead in mortuaries and cemeteries. Why not just take her to a bunch of those places and see what happens. Until you get your license, I'll even drive you, if you want."

"Thanks Mom. That will help a lot." Darcy got up but turned back toward her Mom. "How is Aunt JoAnne and ... her problem. the one you still and she won't tell me about?"

"I really can't, sweetie. It is her story to tell, but I'll say this much. She is about to loose someone dear and is suffering. She doesn't want to talk much about it. She barely talks about it to me, so please don't let her know I've told you even this much, okay?"

"Okay Mom."

Jane did not appear at all that night or the next day.

CHAPTER FOURTEEN

Thursday morning finally arrived but it was hard to be excited about her driver's test without Jane. She had come to rely on Jane to keep her spirits up. However, the written test went smoothly and as she waited for her appointed time to drive, she noticed that her mom seemed even more excited than she was. Darcy began to worry that her mother might start running beside the car shouting encouragement during her test.

Finally it was her time. The examiner directed her into the driver's seat and he sat beside her. "Start your vehicle."

"Well, it's about time. Get this baby moving!" Jane's voice came from the back seat. Good thing only she could hear Jane. Darcy managed not to make any obvious responses to Jane's kibitzing that began to flow nonstop from the back seat. Some of it actually contained valid advice. During the entire test, Jane's commentary was often laced with off-color jokes about the examiners bald head and other ribald topics. Darcy managed to use the helpful and ignore the distracting, passing her test.

Jane's last comment before she disappeared again, finally made Darcy laugh out loud causing the examiner to look at her askance as he gave her the test results. Her mother dropped her off at the school office who were surprised when she presented them with the paper from the DMV, a proper and acceptable excuse for being late, this time. The secretary filed it, gave her the excuse for her teacher of third period, and smiled. "Congrats on you license Darcy."

"Thanks. I waited a bit. Now, I'll need to get a job and then a car." Darcy's emotional high from passing the test did not keep her from worrying about Jane. She thought she saw her for a split second in last period study hall; there and gone, in a blink. Worry kept her from doing any serious school work the rest of last period. Instead, she repeated internet searches for tall red-haired girls who had died. An hour later, she was standing on the sidelines of the soccer field waiting for her turn to try out and show them what she could do.

"Darcy Winters. You're up." The coach said from the field. "Come on out."

She ran out onto the field with as much energy

as she could muster, stopping in front of the coach. "I'm ready."

"Miss Winters, have you played on a team before?" He asked as he looked at his clipboard.

"A few years ago, I played on a church team when I was twelve ... for a while. I also played a lot with friends on the street ... I just really like soccer." She knew that was weak experience and her confidence began to erode as the butterflies in her stomach multiplied. She looked down at the grass and saw Jane's bare feet beside her.

"All right Darcy! Go Darcy! You go get 'em!" Jane hollered from right beside her.

She dared a quick look at her and smiled. Jane seemed okay. With Jane's encouragement, maybe she could do this soccer thing. She looked at the coach. "I'm in good shape, Coach. I'll do better than my experience would indicate."

"Alright then." He raised his stopwatch. "Start with a sprint to the goal and back, twice." Her tryout started. She ran sprints, ran around the field for five minutes, kicked a few goals, and dribbled the ball up and down the field. Jane ran right beside her motivating her with coaching tips on her footwork, demonstrating a deep understanding of the sport. Jane ran and kicked in sync with Darcy, grinning bigger than Darcy had ever seen. Watching Jane's form helped Darcy look better than she had ever looked before.

"Ms. Winters." The coach said as he made a last mark on his clipboard. "You're fast and nimble with great footwork. You'll do well. Congratulations, you on the team for spring practice starting in February."

"Thank you. I'll be ready." Darcy grinned all the way to the bus stop and she knew she looked silly as she continued to grin as she sat on the bench to wait.

Jane sat right next to her and elbowed her in the ribs. "Look at you, wasting all that time as a cheerleader when you could have been playing soccer. You were good, you got skills."

"Ow." Darcy rubbed her side but still couldn't stop grinning. "Not really a waste of time. Cheerleading is a time honored activity for us girls who WEAR CLOTHES."

Jane laughed. "No, seriously. You're actually very good. And I know good." She leaned back on the bench, obviously tired but looking happy and smiling more than Darcy had ever seen. "Man, that was fun. I haven't played soccer since I was twelve before I got too sick to play any more. Since then, I could only watch it on TV. That made me very sad and mad too, but I just couldn't play any more."

"Is that a memory?"

"Yeah, it is. I can actually see myself sitting on a sofa watching TV and feeling hurt and angry that I couldn't play any more." Jane's expression darkened and she hung her head. "In fact, I remember being so ill at home that I was in bed, unable to play anything, even climb stairs ... could only play video games ... feels like not long ago either. I wonder why now with that memory?"

"Wow. A real memory." Darcy thought for a minute. "Could you see anything in the memory that would help us place you somewhere?"

Jane had become translucent and shook her head, her eyes glistening with tears. "Look at me. I guess that even as a ghost, soccer is too much for me. Damn, and double damn!" Jane and her tears faded away.

Darcy knew her mother wouldn't be home until late so she sat down on the big computer in the home office and did more research on her cousin Tabitha. This time she started with basic internet searches using several different popular search engines. She just used her cousin's name. Only three results popped up referencing girls named Tabitha Johnson, but none sounded like her cousin Tabitha. Another search with the first name only, provided many returns. One of the listings spoke of a youth with a first name of Tabitha, living in Canoga Park, who had come all the way from Missouri and was awaiting an organ transplant.

The entry did not mention last names but did mention that her mother's name was Penelope. Darcy figured that with both first names and the

Missouri connection, the article must be about her cousin. She followed a link in that article to an online version of the local newspaper and another article about the need for organ donors for critically ill children.

That article detailed an interview with the mother of a critically sick child in need of an organ transplant. Though there were very few identifying details about mother or child, she felt nervous about reading any further. She didn't want to find out that her only cousin was dead. She grimaced and forced herself to continue reading to the end, despite her fears. And she was glad she did. The conclusion of the article mentioned that the child would be getting a kidney at the local hospital because a donor had finally been found. The date of the article was only a few weeks ago and Darcy figured that she could possibly still be at the hospital. She was sure glad that even regular people could be found on the internet if you knew a few pieces of identifying information.

She looked at her watch, only seven pm, and was struck by a wild idea. On a lark, she left the house and took the bus to the hospital. As she walked into the hospital entrance, she remembered her Mother's anger even at the very mention of her aunt's name, now she was trying to visit her. But Darcy needed more family and her mother was not being as forthcoming as she had promised. Darcy set her jaw and went in.

She told the information desk that Tabitha Johnson was her first cousin whom she hadn't seen in years and she had just heard that she had been in the hospital. If she was still there, she wanted to visit with her and her Aunt Penelope. The receptionist looked on their computer and wrote down a room number and directions, room 664. Being a spy was easy. She grinned, but hesitated outside the door and took a deep breath before knocking. She heard a tired and hesitant voice say, "Come in."

Opening the door slowly, she stepped into the room. The lights were low and she saw a young woman sitting in a recliner beside the hospital bed. "Hi, I'm ..."

"Oh my God! Darcy? Is that you?" The woman jumped out of the chair and ran toward her with her arms out. Darcy tensed up, another hugger. The woman held her and cried for several long moments. Darcy didn't know whether to pull loose or wait. She waited.

Finally the woman released her and then pulled her to another chair and sat her down. "Where's your mother?"

"She's not here. In fact, she doesn't know I'm here, either."

"Well that explains it." She looked sad. "My name is Penelope. I am your father's younger sister and your aunt. Tabitha, over there," She pointed to the bed. "Is ... well ... uh, your first cousin."

"How did you recognize me?" Darcy sat at the edge of her chair, trying to see over the bed rails. Her cousin's red hair was the only thing visible in the high bed from Darcy's position.

"I have a recent photo of you and an old photo of your father." She opened her purse and dug out the two photos. Her dad's photo was an old one from a college yearbook and hers was from last years high school yearbook. "I had to steal the photos from library copies of the yearbooks." She took a shuddered breath. "But, I had no choice because your mother wouldn't give me any pictures."

"Does Mom know Tabitha is in the hospital?" Darcy had wondered about that after she learned of Tabitha's location and considering her mother's reaction to even hearing Penelope's name.

"Oh yes." Aunt Penelope said sadly. "Actually, she knew we were in town for almost a month before my poor Uriah died." Penelope further explained that after Tabitha's kidney transplant, she had been very weak with poor immunity and developed a case of Septicemia. She had floated in and out of a coma like state ever since. The doctors had told her that it wasn't actually a real coma. They called it a minimally conscious state where she almost wakes up sometimes. They said it was better for her than to be fully awake, anyway, because it allowed her body to recover better.

Darcy reached over and offered to take her hand, something she would not have been able to do three weeks ago. Penelope grasped it desperately and took a deep ragged breath. "She's only fourteen, my poor Tabitha. Been sick for the past year." She frowned at Darcy. "How much of our story do you know?"

"Nothing really. Last week was the first time I heard your name and that was all my mother or Aunt JoAnne would say. Didn't know Tabitha existed."

"Your father knew my story .. we had been living in Missouri where I had been sent to have Tabitha; committed actually, by my father, as an unwed teenage mother. The facility was supposed to take us loose women and rehabilitate us into moral, upstanding good women again. The primary method of treatment however, was unrelenting discipline and hard physical labor, unpaid, I might add. The only good things that happened there was Tabitha, and I did get my High School Diploma. But when I turned eighteen, I still had nowhere to go, no home and no family, so I just stayed there and worked on the farm, trying to help the other young girls confined there.

"Just after Tabitha turned eleven, your dad contacted me for the first time since I was thirteen.

That was in 2015 and he rescued me from that farm by sending me money and getting us a place to live in Canoga Park. He had worked through a detective agency because he was already sick and bedridden by 2015. He kept it all a secret from Mary and JoAnne because they were still so very mad at me. Tabitha began to show signs of kidney failure about a year ago and it became life threatening about six weeks ago."

Darcy glanced over to Tabitha, sleeping in the bed. She was already as tall as her own mother, nearly as tall as Darcy was, five-foot-six or seven. Tabitha had her mother's red hair and green eyes. Darcy smiled. Her father's family was genetically strong. "Tabitha looks like you a lot ... and me too."

Penelope stood up and Darcy followed her to the bedside. "She sure does ... Uriah had us move close to him, and then he paid for her to start in a private school. I had hoped that we could eventually become part of the family again. I wanted to be closer to your Dad, my only living relative ... well, living at that time. You know it was your father's kidney that saved Tabitha's life."

Darcy sat back in shock. She knew he had donated his organs but the fact that he had saved Tabitha's life, his own niece, was new information. She looked closer at Tabitha. Her dad's kidney was in her and she smiled. *Guess I didn't see the last of my dad in the ocean after all.*

Penelope stepped closer to the bedside, grasping Tabitha's hand. "After we came here, we then had a nice place to live and Tabitha had a good school but not the thing she wanted most, a father, grandparents, and cousins. Tabitha has never had a family other than me, no one, for all her fourteen years. I was hoping that I could reconnect with your father and maybe you. I figured that Mary and JoAnne would be very difficult and so far I've been right. Until you came tonight."

Darcy listened to her Aunt Penelope as she talked. She definitely understood how Tabitha must have felt with no extended family. Aunt Penelope did not mention anything about Tabitha's father but was obviously desperate to be part of a family again. Penelope's part of the conversation plainly indicated that Darcy's mother and aunt JoAnne did both hate her. But she offered no reasons why that would be the case. Remembering her mother's earlier reaction, Darcy thought it must be true, but that just was not like the woman she knew as her mother or her lonely Aunt Penelope, here in front of here.

Aunt Penelope looked so young, she could be Darcy's older sister and Tabitha could easily be a younger sister. Tabitha looked like Jane, too, maybe a little shorter, and Darcy began to wonder if she could be Jane. She reached into the bed and took Tabitha's hand for a moment and looked closely at her, trying to sense Jane. Though there was that resemblance, there was no presence.

Tabitha was not Jane. But, she still had a cousin and that was a good thing. She hoped her Mother would feel the same way, eventually. She smiled to herself. Patients, asleep or in coma's in hospitals should be her next search like her mother had suggested.

"Aunt Penelope," Darcy said, smiling. It sounded so unusual to say those words. "I need to get home before Mother does, or I'm going to be in deep sh... trouble." After a hug, she hurried from the room but stopped and looked back through the doorway to a sad looking Penelope.

"Please." Penelope said. "Please try to talk to your Mother for me, if you can. I would truly like to see her. Maybe we could work things out. It was a long time ago."

What was a long time ago? What had happened between her mother and Penelope? Darcy rushed to the bus stop, feeling nervous but excited. Her world was expanding. She now had two aunts, a cousin, and an invisible best friend who felt more like a sister.

CHAPTER FIFTEEN

Darcy rushed up to the door and let herself into the house. However, a quiet dark house was not what greeted her. Instead, she heard her mother's angry voice from the well lit living room. "Darcy Marie Winters! Where the hell have you been? No call, no note, nothing!"

Then she heard her Aunt JoAnne. "Mary, she is sixteen after all, give her a little space."

"She hasn't been right since Gary's death, still seeing an invisible girl, still in trouble with the school, and still not cheer leading," her mother said, not quietly. "She already has too much space."

"Mom!" Darcy said as she walked into the living room. "I'm right here. I heard all that!"

"Was it not true?"

"Some of it, and a lot was out of context" Darcy said. Her mother was already clearly upset but she had to tell her about her visit with Aunt Penelope. "Sorry ... thought I would be back before you got home." That much was the truth. "Mom, can we talk? Something serious."

"Sure. At the table. I need a cup of strong coffee. You guys?"

Darcy shook her head no. JoAnne nodded yes.

At the table, coffee in hand, Darcy's mother looked at her. "Me first. Where were you so late?"

"Well, that's actually what we need to talk about." She looked at her mother and aunt, already more family than she had ever had. Now she was going to talk about even more family, but, she was almost sure it would be to an unreceptive audience.

"I was late tonight because I went to the hospital ... to room 664." She waited for a response and she wasn't disappointed. They both looked at her with open mouths and eyes wide with shock. She pressed on despite their obvious surprise. "I had a nice visit with my Aunt Penelope and her daughter, my cousin Tabitha."

"How could you do that?" Her mom turned red and almost sputtered. Darcy had never seen her mom so agitated, so angry.

"Since you guys wouldn't tell me anything after that first mention of Dad's sister, I found out where she was by myself, from the internet, and I went there ... our local hospital. We talked for about an hour." Her mother gripped her coffee cup with rigid fingers, still flush with emotion and Darcy pressed on. "Mom, she seemed real nice and ..."

"Did Penelope ..." JoAnne interrupted. She looked at Mary and then Darcy, her face pale with what Darcy could only interpret as apprehension. "Uh ... Did Penelope mention any thing about me or ... my problem?"

"Only to say that you, like Mom, hated her and had kept her from having a relationship with her only family in the world, my Dad." Darcy turned to face her mother, frustration clearly visible on her face and present in her voice. "What's going on, Mom? I've never seen you this worked up before. What is it with Aunt Penelope? I am sixteen and I need to know. It's my family too."

Her mother sighed, clamping her lips together, and looked at the ceiling. She rubbed her hands on her thighs then rung them together. JoAnne sighed and said, "Damn, Mary, just tell her. It's way past time and you know it."

"Okay, okay." Darcy's mother reached over the table and patted Darcy's hand. "I'm not really mad at you. I understand your curiosity and your need for family. My anger is directed at Penelope for an issue that has been festering within our family for nearly fourteen years."

With the heightened emotions of the moment, Darcy let her mouth work before her brain, again. "Another decades long old issue! What is it with this family and holding grudges!"

JoAnne looked hurt and her mother glared at her. Mary did not respond right away but closed her eyes in resignation for a moment before she continuing. "I guess JoAnne and my elder sister, Hanna, primed us for finding the worst in people. Our guardians for five years didn't help, either. We have always been on guard for someone taking advantage of us."

"Are you saying that Aunt Penelope took advantage of you guys?" Darcy remembered how hurt and lonely she had seemed during the visit.

"When Penelope became pregnant at the tender age thirteen, back in 2003, it was a giant scandal for her family. Her father initially confined her within the family's compound but social services found out quickly and then the local law got involved. Eventually, after several weeks of questioning, she told everyone that it was her brother, your father, who was the father of her baby."

Mary's expression became hard and angry again. "She accused him of child molestation, rape, and incest! She said that he had taken advantage of her on his one and only visit back home in 2003, when your father had gone to see his father who had developed heart problems. Your dad, of course, denied it. JoAnne and I both believed him, though we weren't talking at that time."

Darcy sat with her mouth open. What a terrible

thing for someone to accuse another of. But that didn't fit at all with the sad young woman she had met earlier that evening.

"Everyone believed him. All his friends, even his local community." JoAnne added. "The cops questioned him several times as well as her, and your grandfather. They were the only people living in the home during the alleged time frame."

Mary nodded in agreement. "He was never charged because there was no evidence. Later, an ultrasound of her baby was performed and the baby was determined to be female. Then Penelope just up and disappeared, completely, and your grandfather died a few years later."

JoAnne took a large sip of her coffee and took up the story. "We had assumed that she moved away in shame for blaming her brother, and she did so without even bothering to clear his name first. She left the whole mess wide open, leaving us to deal with the social problems it had created. We didn't know what had happened to her, she never contacted us. Your father, mother, and I, had to move here, to Santa Monica. We had to find a whole new community, just to get away from the stigma Penelope's accusation left in your father's old community. The social condemnation was terrible and we all suffered for years under a cloud of official suspicion."

"Mom," Darcy interrupted. "She didn't run

away. She told me that she had been sent away, committed, by her father to a religious facility for unwed mothers, associated with his church, all the way to Hermann, Missouri. She was forced to live and work on a farm, unpaid, until she was eighteen while raising Tabitha, alone. Sounded like a prison camp to me. Since she had no family who would acknowledge her, she just stayed there after that ... that labor camp, with poor Tabitha."

Darcy noticed that her mother was getting progressively more upset and JoAnne stepped in. "Mary, let me talk."

Mary nodded to JoAnne who continued the story. "We acknowledge that that's a terrible tail about her life, but from our perspective, for eleven years we heard nothing from her, no apology, no hey, how are you, nothing ... not till about six weeks ago, when she came begging your father for a kidney donation. Apparently, Tabitha had developed kidney failure and was dying. She contacted your father on his own deathbed, mind you, and asked for his kidney. What a brazen move! She said it was because he should be a close match for Tabitha. Only then did she finally break down and tell your father the truth about Tabitha. She never told us, who had also suffered so much shame, mind you, just him."

Darcy frowned. That was not the story she had heard from Aunt Penelope. "Mom, that a different story than Aunt Penelope told me. She said that Dad had a detective agency search for her and they had found her back in 2015, just as Dad became bedridden. Dad rescued her from that place right after he had located her. He had sent money for her to move to Canoga Park, just as he became bedridden. She's been around here since then, for three years, hoping for you guys to forgive her."

Her Mother took a ragged breath and shook her head. "Gary never told me ... told us."

JoAnne wiped moisture from her eyes. "Gary always kept trying to do the right thing ... despite us."

Mary wiped her eyes as well. "Shit! Shit! Shit! Our families are so screwed up. Six weeks ago, your Dad did finally tell JoAnne and I what Penelope had told him, the real story of Tabitha's father. Turns out that your grandfather, your dad's father, had raped her ... more than once, until she got pregnant and is Tabitha's father. Of course, your grandfather didn't call it rape. Your Dad is Tabitha's Uncle, but I guess, genetically, a very close uncle, since he is also Tabitha's half brother."

"What? Man, that's just sick! You mean she was only twelve or thirteen when he raped her?" Darcy's heart sank as she thought about her lonely, sad aunt sitting in the hospital. Her grandfather had been a real asshole, no worse. "I can't even think of a word that describes him."

Mary shook her head in agreement. "There is no word that describes the kind of evil he was, but he died long ago, only a few years after Tabitha was born. After Penelope asked for the kidney, your father allowed the blood test to determine his compatibility to be a donor and was a good match. He made immediate arrangements to donate a kidney, but then ..." She looked at JoAnne. "He choose to leave this world on his own terms and donated all his organs. A kidney did go to Tabitha. His heart and lungs went to ... others."

JoAnne picked up the story. "After Gary passed, we considered doing the DNA test for parentage, just to prove the point, but thought better of it. Your grandfather was already long dead and we all knew your father would never have done such a thing. And, of course, Penelope had changed her story, so, we just let it drop."

Mary took Darcy's hands. "Penelope told your Dad that she had been so ashamed about what her father had done to her but because she hadn't seen her brother since she was eight and had hated him for abandoning her, she had accursed him. He would never have forced himself on anyone, let alone a child or his sister."

JoAnne got up for another cup of coffee. "From what Penelope told your father, your grandfather had told her that he wanted a son to carry on the name. All of his sons had died or deserted the family and it was her duty to the family to conceive a son with the Johnson name and blood. In his mind he had no choice and it wasn't rape because she said yes. But his power over her by virtue of fatherhood and his dominate personality was just as strong as if he had tied her to the bed. She had no real choice, not at thirteen. It was rape! But then Tabitha was found to be female during that ultrasound exam when Penelope was 6 months pregnant. He disowned her that day for not bearing a son and she disappeared. But we didn't know he had sent her away."

Darcy thought for a moment. "So Tabitha's my closer than normal first cousin, your and Mom's niece, and she's got one of Dad's kidneys. She developed Septicemia and is very, very ill, in a hospital only minutes from here and maybe dying. And you still haven't been to see her or her mother, a victim of rape and involuntary servitude."

Darcy looked at her mother and aunt. "You guys are way too wound up in the tragic and evil history of Dad's father and all the shit that happened. Tabitha's only fourteen. She is innocent in all of that. Even Aunt Penelope was only a child when she had to suffer rape, and pregnancy, and isolation, and child rearing. You guys had no idea what happened to her for thirteen years. They both need our support, not our condemnation. I'm going to visit them again!"

Her Mom and JoAnne both looked disturbed by Darcy's comment, but before she could continue, Jane spoke from the chair beside her. "Right on! You tell 'em Darcy." Jane began coughing and fell silent again.

Mary and JoAnne looked at each other for a moment and then back at Darcy. JoAnne smiled and Mary made one of her change of direction deep sighs and stood up. She took Darcy up into a great hug. "When did you get to be so smart, mature, and clear headed. I have spent all these years resenting Penelope, even hating her for her accusations and the social problems she created. But you're right, they were all the attempts of a child to make sense of a horrible situation. I'm finding, lately, that I have been so wrong about so many things in my life."

JoAnne joined the hug. "Let's all go to the hospital on Saturday and lend some support."

Mary nodded in agreement. "Absolutely. We need to bring this family together. We have already lost enough."

Darcy felt JoAnne stiffen at her mother's comment and she broke from the hug, shaking with sudden tears. "Yes we have! We've lost too damned much!" She turned and walked upstairs, speaking with her back to them. "I have to go anyway. Got to ... take care ... of ..." She didn't finish and ran up the steps. Mary teared up and followed her upstairs.

Darcy looked at Jane sitting on the sofa, looking as bad as she's ever looked. "Jane? What can I do?"

"Bye Darcy." Jane's eyes rolled back in her head and she slumped forward almost falling off the sofa. Darcy caught her and sat her back on the sofa. Darcy felt this must be near the end ... of something, something big. What was happening to her Jane?

Darcy sat beside her and hugged her tightly. "Stay if you can, but if you can't at least feel me beside you, holding you when you leave. I love you, sister of my heart."

Jane smiled. "Sisters." Her head flopped back and she faded away.

CHAPTER SIXTEEN

Darcy slept fitfully Thursday night, waking up frequently hoping that Jane would have appeared while she slept. Eventually, she could not return to sleep at all. The fear that she would miss Jane, if she only stayed briefly, kept Darcy awake. She dragged herself to school on time Friday morning and participated in class but it was lonely and boring. Concentration was difficult and she rushed home after her last real class, skipping last period study hall.

Darcy's mother and aunt had gone to JoAnne's place to work privately on Aunt JoAnne's terrible personal problem. Darcy ate a microwave dinner and flopped down on the sofa in living room with her laptop but couldn't get started with anything significant. She shook her head in frustration. Even though Aunt JoAnne had moved into the spare bedroom with plans for staying with them for an indefinite length of time, she still had not let Darcy in on her secret problem.

Darcy's mother wanted her to share her Jane issue with Aunt JoAnne, but Aunt JoAnne would not share her problem and it must be severe. Ever since they had decided to go to the hospital the coming Saturday, JoAnne had been nearly a basket case over her mysterious situation that she would not talk about. Darcy understood more than her mother or JoAnne thought she did about grief and loneliness, and Aunt JoAnne's actions spoke of grief to Darcy. Her mother had already said that JoAnne's problem was a problem with or about a person, but who. Did Aunt JoAnne and her mother have another sister or a brother; another Aunt or Uncle? Did Aunt JoAnne have a sick or abusive husband, or a sick child? Darcy wanted to help. After sighing deeply like her mother often did, she decided that Jane's problem was enough for her to handle at the moment. She would be patient with aunt JoAnne's problem and she continued to stare at her laptop screen without actually typing anything.

Late that evening, Jane returned, beginning as an amorphous mist, slowly becoming translucent and finally appearing solid, sitting on the sofa. Darcy whooped out loud and tried to hug her, but Jane didn't waste any time in idle conversation or explanations, waving aside Darcy's welcoming hands. "After you found Tabitha with her transplant situation, I thought a lot about it, but I don't feel that Tabitha is me."

"No, she isn't. I visited with her and touched her and she is not you. She is at least two years younger than you, but she did look an awful lot like you. Oh, and she wasn't naked either."

"Shut up!" Jane managed a thin smile but the effort was too much and it faded. "I had an idea, though. We've already searched about every other category; what about teenage girls with transplants or who are in comas."

Darcy gestured to Jane's body. "Yeah. I thought about that earlier too, but you have never showed those kind of injuries, or scars."

"Can't hurt." She shrugged. "Nothing else has worked. Besides, sometimes I show things, clothes and marks, and sometimes I don't."

"True. Let's do it." Darcy said and did a search on her laptop, not bothering to go to the big machine. They generated a list of teenage transplant recipients for the entire west coast of the US and printed it out.

After bringing the printout back to the sofa, Darcy flopped down in exhaustion. "Jane, I'm falling to sleep. I've got to go to bed. I didn't sleep last night waiting up for you. This will have to wait a few hours at least."

"Sorry. I wish I had at least some control about

when I'm in the gray void, but I don't, not really, and right now, I'm feeling pretty weak myself. I could disappear at any time. I'd better look at the list now while I can. You go on to sleep. I can do it myself. Just lay it on the sofa between us." Jane pointed.

"How can you turn the pages?"

"I'm getting better at touching stuff, but it only works when you have touched it first and you are very near me."

"Alright." Darcy laid the paper down and laid back on the recliner portion of the sofa. "I'll sleep here on the sofa. You can sit beside me. Try to stay. I worry when you're gone."

"Yes, mother." Jane grinned in jest but her eyes were tired and droopy. Darcy drifted asleep just as Jane began reading the list laying between them.

Darcy jumped when her mom shook her awake the next morning, still on the sofa. "You sleep here all night? You're going to regret that later today. Remember, today at noon we're going to the hospital to begin a new era in out family life by including and supporting Penelope and ... more openly supporting Aunt JoAnne. We will need to be especially careful with Aunt JoAnne. She wants to and plans to open up with you about her situation. I hope she does ... can."

Darcy quickly looked at her watch and jumped up, heading upstairs. "Thanks for waking me. I have a cheer leading practice for that makeup game tonight. Even us alternates are required to practice. Be back in plenty of time."

Darcy hurried to school and gave a good performance at practice. She even had friendly conversations with a few other cheerleaders. Jane did not appear at practice to cheer her on and Darcy missed and worried about her, but she got through practice showing off at near her old skill level. Only the captain, Maisie, was not impressed, but Darcy knew she never would be.

Darcy hurried to the locker room after practice, took a shower, dried. She threw her towel over her shoulder, modestly draped down her front, as she walked to the bench in front of her locker and sat down. Without any second thoughts, she began to dress, even with the other girls all around her. Jane still made no appearance to compliment her new comfort levels with being nude. But there was a comment.

"Look at Darcy, getting all bold now, parading around in her birthday suit." Maisie, the squad captain said. "Must be all those invisible naked people she talks to, or maybe she thinking of Robert."

Darcy smiled but made no move to acknowledge Maisie's presence. Little did Maisie know that she was right about the nudity. Jane was responsible for the improvements in her nudity phobia. She chose to ignore Maisie's snide remark about Robert, but Maisie forced the issue and walked over directly in front of Darcy. She leaned in real close, almost nose to nose, holding her own towel between them and glared until Darcy was forced to look up and acknowledge her.

"Nothing you do, nothing you will ever do, will get you back on active status, you wacko. Why don't you just quit?" Maisie's expression dripped disdain and ridicule.

Anger flashed hot through Darcy and before she could think better of it, she reached out and slapped Maisie on her bare backside, hard. The slap reverberated and echoed throughout the locker room, leaving a fire engine red, five fingered, full hand print. Maisie screeched in pain and tears started to stain her clean, showered face. Darcy looked up into her eyes. "Go away, or I'll make it symmetrical. And in case you don't understand that big word, it means I'll slap the shit out of your other ass cheek too. Now, go away!"

Maisie spun around and left, shouting over her shoulder. "You sick weirdo! You'll never cheer again! I'll see to that. Never again! Never! Never!"

Darcy watched the red hand print till it bounced out of sight around corner at the end of the row of lockers. Wow, she had never done anything like that before in her life. Damn, she missed Jane.

"Way to go Darcy!" A couple of other girls

came and sat next to her. "That was great. Of course you will probably have to quit now and never cheer lead again."

The second girl shook her head grinning. "But I'm going to remember that hand print bouncing and wobbling out of sight for a long time. That was really something."

"It was worth it. Thanks. I'm on the soccer team now anyway," she said as she finished pulling on her pants.

"Good for you!" She heard from behind her and quickly glanced. Jane was leaning against the lockers. Her words were encouraging but her expression was serious, almost sick. Darcy's emotional high disappeared and she was worried all over again.

Darcy ignored Jane temporarily and grinned at the other two girls. "I will miss cheering but I have a mystery to solve for my best friend who needs my help. I'll be too busy any way."

"We had you all wrong, Darcy. Good luck." The girls left and Darcy finished getting dressed.

Jane walked out with her. "I don't know what's the matter with me. I feel listless, weak, like that rubber band I mentioned before ... well, it feels like it's getting loose ..."

"Jeez, I hate to see you sick and I want to help you but you know if we solve your problem, you will probably be leaving." Darcy didn't know how she felt about that. Well, actually, she did. She wanted Jane to stay. "You're my best friend... even if you are naked most of the time."

"Me too." Jane leaned over and kissed Darcy on the cheek. "Lets go to the library. I want to do one very specific search based on something I read last night from that list we did about coma victims ... I might have found ... me."

Darcy reached up and felt her cheek. How was she feeling her friend's touch? How was any of this happening or even possible? But now, Jane thinks she has found her self. How can a person feel happy and sad at the same time? She darted into the library, secured a computer, and Jane dictated what to look up; transplant or coma patients, Santa Monica, last eight weeks.

Darcy looked over at Jane, sitting beside her. "You mean, right here in town?"

"Yep." Jane laid her head down for a moment, looking very weak. "There are only four. Two were adult. One was obviously Tabitha with a kidney transplant. Check out that third article about the heart transplant recipient."

Darcy navigated to the newspaper article about a young sixteen year old girl who had been on deaths door for months and who had finally received a last minute heart transplant from a suddenly available local donor on November 2, 2018. But, sadly, she has been in a coma ever since.

The paper did not give her name.

Jane pointed at the text on the screen. "Too young for her name to be made public, but look again at the date of the transplant."

"Oh no." Darcy's attention was captured right away. "That's the same day my father died. Could he be the donor?"

Jane spoke without lifting her head from the table. "We know he was the donor for Tabitha and probably the two adults, why not this other mysterious girl."

Darcy was shocked, but then she straightened up. She shouldn't be shocked. Her father had knowingly donated a kidney to Tabitha and she knew there had been other recipients of his donated organs.

Jane nodded as if she had heard Darcy's thoughts. "How could your mom not have known about another local recipient?" Jane asked.

"Damn!" Darcy spat. "More secrets. My mother knew about Tabitha. She would have had to know about the other recipients unless the hospital was required to keep the recipients of his organs a secret from her. Maybe she just didn't tell me ... mother has been full of secrets." Darcy got up and turned off the computer. "Lets go home. We're going to the hospital at noon anyway. We can find out then for sure."

Jane walked up close beside her. "Darcy, I'm

scared. If it's me, I don't want to be dead and be a ghost forever."

"But you don't want to be memory-less, lost and invisible forever either, do you. We need to ... need to ... I don't know. Let's go, naked Jane."

"Jeez. Stop calling me that. I can't help it."

"Just joking. I'm used to it now, anyway." She swatted Jane on her butt with a loud clap.

"Ow!" Jane skipped ahead a step and they both laughed.

It was good to have the happy Jane back at least for a little while as they rode the bus to the house. Jane began to look look sick as they reached the porch, but stayed present.

Darcy's mother and Aunt JoAnne met them on the porch. "Perfect timing. We were about to go tract you down. Let's go." They got directly into Darcy's mother's car. JoAnne and Mary where silent for the entire ride to the hospital, JoAnne's expression, a mixture of grief and dread. Darcy and Jane followed suite, and remained quiet.

CHAPTER SEVENTEEN

Mary and JoAnne walked up to room 664 with Darcy and Jane trailing behind. Darcy noticed Jane's wide-eyed expression of apprehension and placed her arm around her. JoAnne knocked on the door and waited for an invitation. They heard a sleepy voice. "Darcy is that you?"

Mary looked back at Darcy and nodded to her. Darcy stepped to the door and opened it. "Yes, it's me ... and, I've brought Mother and Aunt JoAnne with me."

They all walked into the room but didn't get very far before Penelope met them on the run, grabbing Mary and JoAnne in a great hug. They responded awkwardly to the intensity of her desperation. Penelope finally disengaged and directed them to chairs. "I can't believe it! Thank you for coming. There's no one else to come if you didn't. We've been so alone. Darcy was our first visitor ... for the whole time Tabitha's been here ... not even anyone from her school." She slumped with exhaustion.

Mary gestured to a chair. "Penelope, sit down. You're exhausted."

"Sorry, not sleeping well in this recliner," she said as she sat on its front edge.

JoAnne and Mary pulled their chairs to either side of her and held her hands. Darcy and Jane walked past the three women and stopped close to the bed. Darcy looked back over her shoulder and asked, "Aunt Penelope. How is Tabitha doing? She still seems awfully deep asleep. Is her infection worse, or her coma?"

"The doctors say it isn't really a coma ... she is still responsive to pain and almost wakes up sometimes. But, I can't rouse her anymore, not with words, not for the past several days." Penelope frowned in frustration. "They are not using tranquilizers either. She is holding her own but the Septicemia is still keeping her dangerously close to organ failure. She hasn't been awake now, even briefly, for four days. I'm so worried." Tears welled up in her eyes and she gripped Mary's and JoAnne's supporting hands even tighter.

JoAnne shook her head and began crying softly. "I truly understand your pain and your fears." She lowered her face into her hands and softly cried. Penelope looked at Mary with a helpless expression. "I don't understand. Has something happened to ..."

"She'll explain later," Mary interrupted nodding toward Darcy.

Jane walked to the other side of the bed and frowned as she stared down at Tabitha. "Damn, we do look a lot alike, but she's not me." Then she reached down and ruffled Tabitha's tightly curled red hair. "Hey! Look at that. I can touch her too. Now that is strange. She's the only other person that I've been able to touch. You guys are cousins, right? Maybe that's why. I feel something pulling me to her, kinda like I do with you."

Darcy looked back at Penelope and sighed. She assumed her mother wouldn't want her to hide her interactions with Jane from Aunt Penelope either. She moved closer to the bedside directly opposite Jane. "Jane. Let me introduce you to Tabitha Johnson, my first cousin on my father's side, Aunt Penelope's daughter. However, she is a much closer than a normal first cousin, because her grandfather was also her father."

"Man, that's sick." Jane said as she gently caressed Tabitha's sweaty face. "You know, I can actually sense her in there. She's a fighter. She is hurting and afraid and lonely too. She wants so badly to wake up. I think she's lost in her own gray nothing."

Penelope looked up sharply at Mary and JoAnne. "You told Darcy that story! How could you?" She buried her face in her hands. "I was only thirteen." Tears and sobs escaped through her fingers.

Mary placed her arm around Penelope's shoulders. "Penelope, just recently ... for nearly the past two weeks, after speaking to a psychologist, we have been working hard to make it a habit to be brutality honest in this family. I've come to realize that partly because of the tragedy of my and JoAnne's early life, we have held accumulated a heavy burden of unexpressed and unresolved anger that we held a secrets."

JoAnne looked up. "Our reaction to you for all these years, was very short-sighted and cruel. We know what happened to you was not your fault and certainly not Tabitha's. Don't be ashamed or embarrassed by it."

Mary took Penelope's hand in both of hers. "There just is not that many members left of this family and if this family is going to survive, it must heal. And the truth is the only path."

"Family?" Penelope said. "I've waited so long to hear that. I've been alone so long."

"Yes, family." JoAnne said and grasped the clasped hands of the others. "We know it's been a long time coming. Please forgive us. But we're here for you, and your daughter, Tabitha now."

JoAnne began to cry and turned her head away to hide her own tears and dropped her hands into her lap, before bending forward and weeping into her hands.

Penelope frowned and looked Mary. "I feel so helpless. I can see that she is hurting. How can I help?"

"She has only shared her pain with me so far. When she can, she will share it with you and Darcy."

Penelope jumped up, startling the others. "Family at last. Truth, too ... okay ... I have been holding a secret since I was thirteen and if I am going to be a member of this new honest family, I must unburden myself of this awful dark secret, must clear the air with some bright truth. Please, listen with an open mind. It's all I ask."

Mary nodded to her cautiously and JoAnne took a ragged breath as she looked up. Darcy looked at her Aunt Penelope and saw her expression; determined and fearful, yet hopeful, all at the same time. Darcy understood the desire to be free of the heavy weight of secrets and waited with the others. She looked at Jane who had not looked up and was still was concentrating on Tabitha.

"Jane?" Darcy whispered. "Did you hear Aunt Penelope? She's about to tell us a secret."

"Trying to reach Tabitha ... in case it works, but yes, I'm listening to your Aunt Penelope as well."

She said.

Penelope turned to face Mary and JoAnne. "I was not raped by my father, as I had told Uriah in 2015 to tell you ... well, not in the common use of that word. My father was truly sick, in body and spirit. I'm sure that Uriah never mentioned this even to you, but our Father had required that sperm samples from each of his sons be stored at a fertility clinic. When Uriah's older brothers were both killed, he discovered that he could not access them as the samples belonged to his sons, not him. He also required it of Uriah before he left for college, but this time he used a clinic that he had influence over through his church congregation. Our father was devastated when Uriah left the family and he was very powerful in the community. He had that clinic ... had them artificially inseminate me with Uriah's sperm in 2003. Uriah is in fact the biological father of Tabitha." Penelope shuddered and took a couple of deep breaths. "I did confirm that to him when I asked him for the kidney, but somehow, he already knew. Neither he nor I had any choice in it."

She briefly covered her face with her hands. "Uriah had abandoned me when I was only eight leaving me alone with our father and his insanity. I was only thirteen when I was inseminated against my will. It felt like a rape to me, and for years I had hated Uriah for abandoning me to my fate. That's why I originally blamed him. I am so sorry for that now, but I was only a frightened, angry child."

Neither Mary nor JoAnne said anything in their shock for several long moments. Penelope began to shift her feet in apprehension. Mary stood up and opened her arms. "Welcome to the family. The pain of truth will set us all free. And there is pain and guilt enough to go all around."

JoAnne joined the hug and Darcy shook her head, shocked at the depravity of her grandfather, but in awe with the idea that her cousin was actually her sister. She actually had a sister. Wow. The truth was powerful and maybe her mother was right. Then she noticed that Jane still had made no move to leave Tabitha. Jane still held Tabitha's hand and was caressing her face. "Jane, everything okay? What have you sensed?"

"I heard your aunt Penelope. So you and Tabitha are actually sisters. That must be why I sense her so strongly, just like I do you. She's a real fighter. I sense her struggling to wake up, to find a way out of the nothingness. Grab her other hand and talk to her. Maybe she'll hear you." Jane leaned over and kissed Tabitha's sweaty forehead.

Darcy looked back at her mother, JoAnne, and now Penelope, who were staring at her and her seemingly one-sided conversation. She sighed and began explaining. "Jane is here, on the other side of the bed. She says that Tabitha is struggling to wake up and is a fighter." She grabbed Tabitha's hand and leaned in close. "Tabitha. My name is Darcy, Darcy Marie Winters. I'm your sister and I swear, we look almost like twins. I know you've been sick, but it's time to wake up. Take control in your mind, find my voice and come toward me. I want us to be a family. The time of being alone is over." Darcy looked up at Jane. "Jane, you can touch her. Maybe she can hear you too. Say something out loud to her."

Jane concentrated and placed her hand under Tabitha's head then she leaned in and touched her forehead to Tabitha's. "Hi, Tabitha. My name is ... uh, Jane. I am a spirit, but somehow I can touch you, just like I can touch your sister, Darcy. Please hear my voice and wake up, your mother is so worried. We all are." She kissed her forehead again.

Darcy looked back at her mother and aunts. Obviously, neither her mother nor Aunt JoAnne had explained to her shocked looking Aunt Penelope about her invisible friend, Jane. More family truth will be needed, soon.

Tabitha's eyelids began to flutter and her breathing quickened and deepened. Darcy and Jane leaned back a little just as her bright green eyes popped opened and she coughed, looking at Darcy. "I heard you. Darcy Winters. Sister? You'll have to explain that one to me. Mother never told me that!" She took another deep breath. "Where is Jane?"

Darcy heard gasps and chairs scrapping from behind her as Penelope jumped up. Before she acknowledged the fast approaching Aunt Penelope, she frowned in surprise at Tabitha and pointed to the other side of the bed.

Tabitha turned her head toward Jane. "It was you I heard first. Thank you so much for ... hey, why are you naked?"

Jane's eyes widened in shock. "You can see me?"

"Yeah, every naked inch of you." She laughed a little. "But I felt you first, in my head. Felt you kiss my forehead. Your touch reached me first and I kept following it up through that awful gray mist till I finally heard Darcy's voice."

Darcy laughed. "I'll fill you in on the naked Jane story later, okay?"

"Hey!" Jane frowned. "Enough with the naked Jane shit? I can't help it."

Darcy looked behind her as her mother and Penelope reached the bed. JoAnne was still sitting with her head buried in her hands and had missed Tabitha's awakening. But Mary and Penelope had not. They were staring at Tabitha. Penelope pushed past Darcy to the bedside and grabbed Tabitha. "My God. Your awake. I was so worried." She began pressing the nurse call button and demanding a doctor right away. "Tabitha is awake!" She informed the nurse several times.

"Darcy and Jane woke me up." She pointed at each, as far as she was concerned.

"Darcy and who?" Penelope asked, looking around.

Darcy's Mom stepped up beside Penelope. "Darcy sees and talks to an invisible friend called Jane. Apparently, Tabitha sees her too."

Tabitha grinned, reaching over and grabbing Jane's hand. "That's right. Not invisible to me. I can see her and I can hold her hand too. See." She lifted Jane's hand but it looked like she was lifting air to the adults.

Tabitha looked back and forth between Jane and Darcy and grinned. "Mom. Guess what? Invisible Jane has beautiful red hair and green eyes just like me and Darcy. I heard both of them talking to me but it was Jane who first found me in that awful gray emptiness and helped me find my way."

Mary shook her head. "Penelope. Just accept it ... for now. We'll explain more later."

Tabitha looked at her mother, her expression quizzical. "Mom, what's this about Darcy being my sister, not my cousin?"

JoAnne stood up with an anguished moan before Penelope could frame an answer and everyone turned toward her. Her face was unreadable, almost unrecognizable with stress. "Seeing Darcy every day for the past two weeks with beautiful her red hair and green eyes, then seeing Tabitha, today, with her wonderful red hair and green eyes has been beyond difficult for me. Now, I hear Tabitha say that even Darcy's invisible friend Jane, has gorgeous red hair and green eyes ... it's all just too much."

She broke down into great sobs slumping as Mary and Penelope went to her and supported her back into the chair. Darcy, Tabitha, and Jane watched from the bed.

JoAnne supped a few times before clearing her throat. "Tabitha's description of Jane forced me to remember a decision that I came here today to make, a decision that I have been avoiding. I haven't been able to even process it in my head or my heart ... what has to be decided for my own daughter just down the hall in room 667. She had a transplant too, her heart."

Jane and Darcy looked up in alarm.

JoAnne looked up into each of the their eyes, around the room. "I have to decide today, whether to pull the plug on my only child, my beautiful red haired, green eyed daughter, or to watch her continue to exist day after day as part of those damned life support machines." Sobs overrode any further words and she buried her face in her hands.

Darcy and Jane looked at each other, both frowning. Suddenly, Darcy had a terrible, hollow feeling and from Jane's expression, she could tell that she shared the same feeling. As with a single mind, they left Tabatha's bedside and quietly walked past the grieving mothers toward the door.

"Darcy, where are you going?" Her mother asked, looking up.

Ignoring her mother and the questioning expressions of the others, she darted from room 664 and almost ran down the hall to room 667, Jane right beside her.

CHAPTER EIGHTEEN

The door to 667 was open and there were no nurses in the room. Jane and Darcy ran through the doorway, heading straight to the bed. They stopped at the bed's railings and gazed at the bank of machines that surrounded the head of the bed in a giant "U" shape. The array of mechanical and electronic devices reminded Darcy of her father's machines. There were wires and tubes all over the patient, whose face was barely visible under the elastic bands and tape.

Darcy lowered the railing so she and Jane could lean into the bed and peer more directly at the patient's face. Jane gasped, standing straight up with her hand over her mouth. She collapsed forward onto the mattress, catching herself with both hands, visibly shaking. Darcy leaned in and gasped as well. Her invisible, naked friend Jane was the same person that was in the bed. Jane had found her physical self.

"That's me!" Jane said, hesitantly reaching toward the patient's hand, laying motionless beside the body. She turned towards Darcy standing beside her. "Darcy, thank you for being the sister of my heart."

She touched her own hand and immediately began to fade. Tears streamed down her face as she continued to become more and more translucent, finally, actually looking like a wispy ghost. "Darcy, I'm going for good this time. I can feel it. Don't forget about us. Don't let them pull my plug. I'm still in there! Don't let me die! Darcy, I love you."

"I love you too! Hold on! Don't go." Darcy reached for Jane's hand for one last touch but Jane was gone and Darcy's hand landed on the hand of the girl in the bed. That hand was limp but it still felt like Jane. It was Jane. Darcy grasped it, sobbing, falling forward onto the bed over their clasped hands.

"Darcy Marie Winters!" Her mother's voice suddenly intruded into her grief from the doorway. "What are you doing in here?" Her mother rushed into the room, followed by JoAnne.

Darcy turned from the bed and stifled her sobs enough to speak as she lifted Jane's hand from the bed. "This is Jane ... Jane's physical self. This is my invisible best friend, right here in this bed."

JoAnne rushed to the opposite side of the bed and reached through the wires and tubes to grasp her daughter's other hand. JoAnne's face was streaked with previous tears and her eyes were red and puffy. She stared silently at the girl in the bed as Mary came up beside her and placed her arm across her shoulders.

"Your daughter is such a beautiful girl. She looks just like my Darcy and Penelope's Tabitha."

"Darcy," her Mother said from across the bed. "This is Charlotte Christina Annabelle Baker, JoAnne's daughter, your ... first cousin. She was the recipient of your fathers heart. But she never woke up after the surgery. Some problem with the anesthesia, they assume."

"Well, she is also my Jane and I want her back!" Darcy began to crawl into the bed.

"Darcy! What are you doing? Get down from there!" Her mother said and reached across the bed to stop her.

Darcy shook off her mother's grasp and despite her mother's demands to stop, Darcy finished crawling up into bed, sliding through and around the maze of wires and tubes until she settled next to her best friend. She wiggled her arm under Jane's neck and pulled her close. "Jane, please come back to me. I've never had a friend before like you, and I don't mean naked."

JoAnne finally looked up as the monitors began

beeping and saw where Darcy was. "Darcy, get down from there, right now. Please ... she dying. Let her go in peace."

"NO!" Darcy shouted. "She's not dying. I won't let her. She's still in there! I know it! I spoke to her only a minute ago. She can't die. You can't let her!"

Nurses began rushing in as more of the machines began to sound alarms. "You! Out of that bed." One of them shouted.

Darcy concentrated on Jane and ignored the wild scene around her. Her mother was shouting. The nurses were shouting. Her Aunt JoAnne was crying hysterically, while more and more of the machines began to beep and chirp and clang. The breathing machine, however, continued its repetitive clump and whoosh unchanged, as it pushed air into the comatose girl named Charlotte, Darcy's naked Jane.

Darcy kept talking and begging between her own bouts of tears. "Jane, Jane, please don't die, please don't let your body die, don't stay like this, come back to me. I need you. Jane!"

"Who is Jane?" A nurse asked.

JoAnne reached across Charlotte to Darcy. "Darcy, please! This is not Jane. Her name is Charlotte, my dying daughter, your ..."

"Call security." A nurse came up beside Darcy and began to pull at her. "What are you doing to her? Listen to the alarms. You're disturbing the patient! Get down now!"

JoAnne looked up from across the bed. "Nurse. It's okay. She can't hurt her. My Charlie is already dying. Darcy is her ... cousin and is just grieving and confused."

"It's against hospital protocol. She needs to get down."

JoAnne burst out into tears. "I said my Charlie is already dying! Let us be! Get out!" The nurse backed up and made a quick scan of the various alarms that were going off, beginning when Darcy had crawled into the bed. Charlie's heart rate and blood pressure were continually rising. "I'll be back in a few minutes. She's disturbing the patient."

Darcy took little notice of her mother, JoAnne, or the nurses until her mother said. "Darcy, this whole crazy scene is hurting your Aunt JoAnne. Listen to me! Please look at her face."

Darcy's mother stepped closer to the bed beside JoAnne. Darcy finally looked up through her own tearful eyes, across Jane, to the tortured face of her Aunt JoAnne who was still standing by the side of the bed holding Jane's hand. Darcy's mother spoke softly. "Charlie almost died before the transplant and then several times after the surgery. Something happened with the anesthesia and now she is just fading away, weaker and weaker, every day since. Charlie has slipped too deep into the coma. Darcy, she is gone. She is alive only with these machines.

Aunt JoAnne is here today trying to prepare herself for Charlie's death, like we had to do for your father. We need to let her go, Darcy."

"NO!" Darcy screamed and hugged Charlotte tighter. "I won't loose her too."

"Darcy, honey. Don't make this more difficult than it already is for JoAnne." Mary said softly, crying now as well.

JoAnne laid her head on the Charlie's other shoulder, tears wetting the gown and sheet. "Mary! I can't do it! I just can't let her go! She was my whole life!"

Darcy pulled her face closer to Jane's and spoke directly into her ear. "Remember the first time you found me in the library when you were so lost and confused. Then somehow you found me again at the bus stop, and then again in my shower. You always found me, no matter where I was. And it was the best thing that had ever happened to me in my entire life. Please hear me now. Hear my voice, feel my touch, sense my love. Find me again, please, please! I need you!" She began to sob as she hugged Charlie, but she was still Jane in her heart.

Mary reached across and grabbed Darcy's shoulder in support while JoAnne continued to cry on Charlie's other shoulder. Mary waved the security and nurses away, again. "Go away! Let us grieve in peace. Unplugging can wait a little longer." Several nurses left but one nurse remained by the door nervously eyeing the readouts and making notations.

Darcy became aware of it first, a tiny shudder. As she held Charlie tight, Charlie shivered with a movement too small to see, but Darcy felt it. Then there was another and another. Finally, Charlie's head shot back as she tried to take a large gulp of air around the endotracheal tube. She began to gasp and struggle to breath, but with the tube still in place, she began to gag and choke, fighting the automatic breathing machine.

"Oh my God! She choking!" JoAnne jumped and hollered. "Nurse!"

Charlie's eyes flew open, wide with panic. She coughed and gagged and thrashed in her efforts to breath. The nurse ran from the doorway and immediately begin to, unceremoniously, remove the breathing tube, before Charlie hurt herself in her efforts to breath. As the long tube was pulled from her throat and trachea, Charlie gurgled and retched and thrashed even more. Darcy could not move off the bed in time and just tried to lay back out of the way.

With the tube finally out, Charlie finally stopped struggling for air and her eyes gradually focused. She turned her face toward Darcy, their noses practically touching, and croaked with her long unused, real voice. "Love you." Her voice was hoarse.

Darcy was crying and made no move to get up, or even loosen her grip on her Jane's neck, but leaned in and whispered through her tears, "I guess, I can't call you naked Jane any more, Miss Charlotte Christina Annabelle Baker."

Charlie laughed weakly. "Jeez, you know my full name. Just call me Charlie ... and not naked Charlie either." She laughed again and coughed as she began to look around. "Mom?" She called out, but her voice was barely a whisper.

JoAnne finally found her own voice and stopped staring. "It's a miracle! Charlie! I can't believe it. You're alive!" She threw her arms around her, the wires, and even Darcy in her enthusiasm. "I don't understand. You were gone."

"Not gone, Mom, just lost. Darcy helped me find my way back," she said.

"Darcy, get down now," Mary said as she also tried to move JoAnne back from the bedside so the nurses could work. "Let the nurses check her out and straighten her up a bit."

Darcy didn't want to let go but reluctantly slid out from under the tubes. The nurses began removing tape and leads and the breathing machine, eventually leaving only the fluid IVs, the urinary catheter, and the heart monitor in place. JoAnne would not completely leave her side or even release her hand, forcing the nurses to worked around her. They just grinned. Darcy stood back from her side of the bed, waiting her chance to climb back on.

When the nurses left after the first round of clean up, Darcy sat on the bed beside Charlie while JoAnne looked back and forth from one to the other, frowning. "So, Darcy, how do you know my Charlie so well? You speak as if you're the best of friends."

Darcy sighed like her mother does and looked at Charlie. "It's complicated."

"Make it simple, then, just the basics," JoAnne said as she sat down next to the bed.

Darcy looked at he mother for help but got only a shrug. "I never heard of Charlie before ... but I knew that Jane's body was most likely in the hospital. I knew that because Jane and I had done internet searches and found an article in an online paper about a teenager, near death, in desperate need of a heart transplant. She had been granted a second chance by a suddenly available perfect match donor heart. And with the dates of Dad's death matching the suddenly available donor, we wondered if Dad was the donor. We also figured that that recipient was probably my Jane ... well, her body, in a coma."

"You and Jane, your imaginary friend, read about my Charlie." JoAnne said, frowning. "That doesn't explain how you know her."

"Give me a chance. I'll get there," Darcy said.

"Mom," Charlie interrupted. "It was me. I

helped Darcy. I was Jane."

JoAnne finally wiped her tears. "That can't be. You were in a coma so deep we were out of options. We were here today to ... we were only minutes away from letting you go!" She burst into wails and Mary comforted her.

"Let me go! Mom? Were you really going to do it?" Charlie asked, her voice still raspy with lack of use.

"You were dying," JoAnne said, "sinking, every day, further and further beyond recovery, deeper into the coma. We had to put a tube in your stomach to feed you. The breathing machine was working for you more and more each day. The doctors were sure you would never rouse. We were going to have to pull your plug and let you go peacefully."

"My body may have been in serious trouble, in this bed, but my spirit was just lost and running around in a gray nowhere universe till I found Darcy." Charlie tried to sit up but lacked the energy. "I was Jane, Mom, or my spirit was. It was me that Darcy was seeing these past weeks."

Darcy looked up sharply in shock with a belated realization. "Aunt JoAnne! I guess with the stresses of the last few minutes, I haven't been paying attention, but if you're Charlie's mother and you're my Aunt, then ..."

"That's right. You guys are ... uh, first cousins."

JoAnne nodded somewhat subdued.

Darcy grinned and threw her fist into the air. "Alright! Our family just got bigger again. I now have a sister, Tabitha, and a first cousin, Jane, I mean Charlie."

Mary looked at her suddenly pinging phone. "Message from Penelope," she smiled at JoAnne and read it aloud. "The doctor is in with Tabitha now. She seems to have completely turned a corner. Thank God."

Mary texted back, "Our hearts are full for you, Penelope. A miracle has happened here as well. JoAnne's daughter, Charlie, has also come back to us, apparently fine. We'll come as soon as possible."

CHAPTER NINETEEN

The nurses brought the head of the bed up, allowing Charlie to get into a more comfortable reclining position where she could see the others better. Darcy got back on the bed and sat beside her, unwilling to be separated. It felt good to know that Charlie, Jane, was alive and finally visible to all.

Darcy's mother pulled up chairs for herself, and JoAnne. "Time for more straight talk, time to free all the skeletons in our closet. Let me start with this. Darcy, your dad had always wanted to donate his organs when he died. We had talked about this even before we were married. But last month, we found that he was a perfect match for Charlie here, as well as for Tabitha."

"But my Charlie never woke up from surgery," JoAnne added, still tearing lightly, then she looked up, frowning. "And Tabitha got an infection, right?

Weird. Both of them."

"Septicemia." Darcy said, nodding. "Aunt Penelope said that her coma like sleep had worsened till Jane and I helped her wake up only a few minutes ago. I mean Charlie. Guess that's why the doctor is in with her now."

Mary frowned. "Well, it wasn't your father's organs that made them sick. The individuals who received the other kidney and lungs, recovered nicely and are just fine."

Charlie heaved a big sigh, exercising her chest muscles for herself for the first time in weeks. "And I'm awake now too, like Tabitha. Nurse, can you get some more of these tubes out of me." She lifted her covers but slammed them right back down, her face blanched pale. "Damn! I am naked Charlie!"

"Of course you are." Darcy laughed. "I guess somethings will never change."

"Oh, shut up," Charlie said, then frowned and peeked back under the covers at herself. There were pickups stuck around her breasts, a feeding tube and port stitched into her stomach, a catheter and plastic tube exiting her most private area, and wires attached to her toes. Next, she twisted around a bit and looked at her backside. "Darcy, look at this." She raised the sheet for Darcy to look and pointed to the gastric tube. "Remember when that happened?" Then she raised the cover a little from the side and rolled over to show her butt cheek with a big red hand print. "How about that? You popped me a good one earlier today at school. I'll remember that, you brute. But how it shows up here, on my real butt, I don't understand. How could that happen? How could that mark transfer to my real body?"

Darcy shrugged. "How could any of this happen?"

Both mothers where looking at them with questioning frowns. JoAnne finally said, "Charlie, put that sheet back down. You have no clothes on. You two seem awfully familiar with each other ... how do you girls know each other, again? Tell me with details this time, so it makes sense."

Mary frowned. "Yeah, Darcy. You seem awfully relaxed about her nudity. You over all that now?"

Darcy frowned. "We already told you. Charlie is Jane ... well, was Jane, my invisible, naked friend. And I am much more comfortable with nudity ... under the right circumstances, because of her."

"That's good," her Mother said. "But we still need an explanation that make sense to us for how you know each other ... so well. And an imaginary friend, won't do."

"Mom. Jane was never imaginary. She was a spirit. She was Charlie's spirit, that came to me as her body lay here in the hospital." Darcy held Charlie's hand and frowned at he mother. "I thought you were okay with my Jane. You said before, that you would try to understand my invisible friend Jane and that I should be truthful about her. And I was."

Darcy held up Charlie's hand and looked at her mother and then her Aunt. "Charlie, here, is the real, physical girl whose spirit was my invisible naked friend. That's the only explanation I have. Jane, help me out here ... I mean Charlie."

Charlie took a deep breath, still finding it a little difficult. "It's a long and unbelievable story. Darcy, you start and I'll jump in when I first appeared in spirit form. Okay?"

Darcy shook her head. "Why don't you start. It's really your story."

JoAnne frowned and smiled at the same time. "Well, somebody start ... and soon, before we all die of old age."

Charlie almost laughed then straightened her covers, patting them down at the edges assuring that her nakedness wasn't too obvious. "Yeah. Okay. From the beginning, but it's going to sound real crazy."

Charlie sat up straighter. "Now that I remember everything, let me start back when I got so sick ... before the hospital. My heart was enlarged and I had so little energy, I could do almost nothing but play video games and watch TV. Then I ended up here in the hospital waiting for a transplant, Right,

Mom?"

"Yes, that's true. Then, on November 2, you received a heart ... Darcy's father's." JoAnne said.

"I did not know Darcy before I got sick." She frowned pointedly at Mary and then her mother. "But I should have. I knew OF her, of course, the cousin that I could never see, could never know, and who would never know that I even existed ... but I guess that's another family story." She took several deep breaths before continuing. "Actually, I remember being sick for a while, years, before it got bad. I was near death for the week before the transplant surgery, right here in this hospital. I barely remember being wheeled to the operating room ... then nothing for what seemed a long while."

Darcy reached over and took her hand. "I wish I had known you then. I would have been here to help you."

Charlie smiled. "The next thing I remember was a whole lot of pain and my entire world was gray, just an endless expanse of gray nothing. I was so lost and scared, just floating in that nothing, not even sound in there."

JoAnne nodded her agreement but frowned with questions. "Don't know about the gray world. You never woke up in recovery. In fact you have lain in that bed from then until a few minutes ago, except for the time needed to perform a few minor surgical procedures, installing that feeding tube and once when they did a diagnostic catherization of your new heart."

"Well," Charlie said. "That's not how I remember my time. At first all I felt was pain. I was lost in a that damn fog, still racked with pain. I had no idea where, who, or even what I was. I cried and screamed for someone to rescue me, to find me, even to just talk to me. Then, suddenly I opened my eyes and I was in a room full of books beside a freaked out, red haired girl who was screaming at me about putting on clothes. She had actually seen me and that meant I did exist. Then poof, back in the gray hell. Then poof, I keep appearing in other places but always near that same red headed girl. No one else could see me, only her. But she talked to me and screamed at me, but she saw me. That funny girl who was so put out by my nakedness and who puts on her nightgown before taking off her towel ... was Darcy."

"TMI." Darcy grunted. "I got better ... well, anyway, this naked girl that kept appearing beside me, couldn't remember anything, not even her own name, so I named her Jane. After a couple of weeks of this coming and going, we actually became the best of friends. We figured that Jane was a trapped ghost and began researching the internet, trying to find who she had been. We eventually ended up looking at coma patients, and ended up here."

Charlie wriggled into a better sitting position. "When I saw my body laying in this bed, I was sucked right in, back into the gray hell. But this time I could hear Darcy calling me from far away and I scrambled toward her voice till I woke up, only a few minutes ago."

Darcy hugged her. "Those were the longest few minutes in my life."

"Me too, but I heard you and when I got close to waking up, I heard Mom and Aunt Mary." Charlie looked at her mother. "When I woke up, I remembered everything from my life before, including what I saw and did as that naked spirit, Jane. Anyway, while I was a free and embarrassingly naked spirit, was when I actually met Darcy for the first time ... one week after the surgery." Charlie's expression, dared anyone to question her.

"Not possible, dear. You were in a coma, in that bed, naked, with tubes all over you. How could you two have met?" JoAnne looked at Mary for support. Mary only shrugged.

"Well, Mom, my naked body may have been here in this bed ..." Charlie started.

"But her naked spirit was visiting me." Darcy said. "I was in a lot of trouble at school and in my head, when suddenly I see this naked girl sitting near me in the library. Then, no matter where I went or what I did she'd be there, almost always naked."

Charlie laughed. "Yeah, naked like I was here, but at that time, I didn't remember anything from my life, just some general feelings. I only seemed to even exist when I was close to Darcy. Near her, I felt less afraid, and less alone." She looked at Darcy. "I never said thank you ... thank you for overcoming your prudish phobias and becoming my friend when I needed it so much."

"Shut up, you naked ninny." Darcy grinned and looked at her mother. "Like I told you before, she didn't remember her name, so I called her Jane. She appeared everywhere, always embarrassing me with her nakedness. She even popped in several times while I was naked. I almost passed out with shame."

"Yeah!" Charlie sat up straighter, laughing. "You should have seen it. Did you know Darcy can even blush on her butt. Never saw that before."

Darcy glared at Charlie until she stopped laughing. "Well, anyway, after a while, I realized that there was a real person inside all that naked skin, a lonely and lost person, one that I quickly learned to love like a sister."

Mary and JoAnne smiled at each other as they listened to Charlie pick up where Darcy left off with their incredible story. "Darcy helped me find myself and drug me up from the hell I was in, apparently just in time, too." Charlie grinned. "Mom, I'm so sorry that you had to suffer so much. I really tried to come back, but without Darcy, I wouldn't have made it."

Mary and JoAnne looked at each other. With a sigh, they exchanged a look, an understanding, and an acceptance, but neither interrupted the story.

Darcy put her arm around Charlie's shoulders. "Over the past weeks, we became like sisters. She slept in my bed most nights, I think. She even came to school with me and sometimes watched you make breakfast, Mom."

Charlie smacked her lips. "No one could see or hear me except Darcy and I wanted to eat those breakfasts so bad, but I couldn't touch anything, anyway. Amazingly, after a while, even though I was only a spirit, Darcy and I could touch each other and we both felt the touch. It was sort of like magic or something." Charlie said as she stretched, causing her sheet to suddenly slip down her chest to her stomach."

Darcy grabbed the sheet and replaced it laughing. "Hey! No more of that nakedness sh... stuff. You got to work on that."

"Shut up."

Darcy's mother raised both her hands for them to stop. "I don't know how to rationalize your stories, so I will just accept it. JoAnne, I suggest you do the same. But there is something else that may also be at play here."

Mary sighed one of her signature sighs and faced JoAnne. "JoAnne, time for more gut wrenching family truth. Penelope let her secret out and now it's time for you and me to do the same. It's time to clear our closets of skeletons and drag out those family secrets into the light of day. JoAnne, you're up. Tell them. You know it's time."

Mary turned to the girls on the bed. "Darcy, Charlie, listen carefully. This is important."

Darcy looked at Charlie and then at her mother and her aunt. "More secrets about me or Charlie?"

Darcy's Mom nodded. "About the whole family in general, but mostly more detail about Charlie's story." Her mother answered. "JoAnne?"

"Mom?" Charlie asked. "What's she taking about?"

"Are you sure, Mary?" JoAnne looked almost frightened, ignoring Charlie's question.

"Mom?" Now Charlie looked alarmed.

Mary nodded and JoAnne sighed. "Charlie. Please listen to me with your heart and don't judge me or your Aunt Mary too harshly ... please don't hate me."

Charlie frowned and sat up straighter. "Mom. I could never hate you."

"We'll see." JoAnne lowered her face and spoke to the floor. "Darcy's father was indeed the perfect donor match for you ... because he was also your father."

Charlie's mouth dropped open and she gulped a couple of breaths. "What do you mean, my father?"

"I mean, he was your biological father."
JoAnne still could not look up from the floor.

Darcy's eyes widened with the memory of
being told about JoAnne's affair with her father.
From Charlie's expression, Darcy could see that
Charlie had no knowledge of the affair.

Charlie said "I don't understand. How could
that be?"

JoAnne grimaced. "Charlie, you're sixteen. You
know how that can be."

JoAnne looked up directly at Charlie's eyes.
"Gary and I had a short affair while Mary had
become pregnant with Darcy ... and I got pregnant
with you. When I told him I was pregnant, he told
Mary about the affair and about my pregnancy. He
and I broke it off and Mary and he stayed together.
But, for the next thirteen years, Mary and I barely
spoke and we kept our families apart in our anger
and resentment ... one of the greatest errors of our
lives!"

Charlie's eyes widened in shock. "That affair,
right. I remember Aunt Mary telling Darcy about it
at breakfast one day."

JoAnne frowned. "What? How?"

"I was Jane then." Charlie replied without
embellishment.

JoAnne stood up and walked to the bedside
opposite Darcy. "Anyway, from the moment he
found out about you, he made sure you were

covered on his medical insurance, and he provided for you for the rest of his life. He made sure you attended the best schools. He paid for all your music lessons, all your field trips, your school uniforms, anything you needed, from that day on. However, Mary and I, in our anger with each other, forced him to agree to never see you, never be in your life." She covered her face with her hands.

Charlie finally got her mouth working. "I had a father who supported me my whole life, and you never told me?" Her voice was loud with hurt, tinged with anger.

"Yes." JoAnne answered, like a deflated balloon and started to cry. "Mary and I, and he, agreed that you could never see or even know about him. I was never to give him pictures of you or anything, and I didn't. Then Mary and I agreed never to see each other again and I could never see him again. We broke our family apart in anger and resentment and filled our closets with the skeletons of our secrets, to decay and smell and make the rest of our lives sick and lonely."

CHAPTER TWENTY

Mary looked at Darcy and then Charlie before grabbing JoAnne in a hug of support. "The details are true, like she said, but this whole nasty mess does not fall solely on her head. I knew all of this, the affair and about you, Charlie. Back then, I never questioned what we were doing, keeping our families apart. I was so blinded by my anger at your father and JoAnne's betrayal. I never considered the damage it was doing or the pain it was causing."

Charlie looked at her mom through her own tears. "I wanted a father so bad growing up. All those father daughter events that I was too embarrassed to go to with you. Always wondering why the man who made me, could not even take the time to write me a letter. You never even told me he helped support me my whole life. That would have at least been something. I can't believe you did that." She leaned her head on Darcy's shoulder.

Darcy looked at her Mom and Aunt JoAnne for a moment and then back at Charlie. Tears of sympathy, compassion, and vicarious guilt pooled in her eyes. "I'm sorry our family did that. He should have been your father too. He should have been in your life. We should have been in each others life. I would have loved to have shared him with you, sister" Darcy leaned her head on Charlie's and took her hand.

Darcy sat up suddenly. "In fact, I wrote a message to him when we spread his ashes in the Pacific. I didn't know we were real sisters then, but I told him about you and how we were sisters of the heart ... will you still be my sister now, even with all that family drama in our past?"

Charlie squeezed Darcy's hand and grinned through her tears. "Let's not make the same mistakes our parents did, though. Sisters forever ... as long as I can stay dressed."

JoAnne looked up at Charlie, frowning, and Charlie laughed. "Mom. Remember, when I was a spirit visiting with Darcy, I was always naked, all the time, everywhere. Course only Darcy could see me. Hell, I'm still naked now under this sheet, even here in the real world."

Mary walked over to the bed. "Charlie, for my part in those decisions for your father to ignore you, please forgive me. Your mother, your father, and I, all ignored family on both sides and I now know we were so wrong. I know that ignoring you hurt him all these years even before he got sick."

Mary offered to take Charlie's hand and she took it. "But maybe this will help ... when your father became aware of just how serious your condition was, he made a decision ... to terminate his life support early, so his organs could be available to you in time to save your life."

Charlie eyes widened and the color drained from her face. "He didn't. He died for me? I didn't know that." She looked at her Mom. "You never told me that 'my donor' had chosen to die in order to give me this heart."

Mary squeezed her hand. "Actually, there were four young people given a chance at life because of his organs. You, Tabitha, and two others. Your mother was going to tell you after you recovered. She thought it would make it difficult for you, if you knew that detail during your recovery. Your father had been on total life support for almost three years, even more complete than yours. But, unlike you, he could never have gotten better. He was living on borrowed time, completely at the mercy of machine and medical support. He was a prisoner in his own mind. He could have possibly prolonged his life a year or two, but he believed that your life, and Tabitha's was much more important than extending his ... and I signed the papers with him.

Your mother was also fully aware of his decision, as was Penelope for that matter.

Charlie let Darcy take her other hand and she started crying. "I wish I had known him."

JoAnne slowly stepped forward, pulling out a folded piece of paper from her purse and handed it to Charlie. "Your father had dictated this to the hospital legal staff when he registered his living will with them, just before he became totally dependent on life support. The hospital gave it to me when he passed. It's to you ... from your father to you. I was to give it to you when you were well enough. But you never woke up ... until now. I couldn't bring myself to read it. I had already lost him and I was loosing you too."

Charlie took the tear stained folded paper and tore the seal that held the folds together but she closed her eyes, the paper quivering in her shaking hands as she unfolded it. She looked past the paper to her mother, her aunt, and then her sister. "In honor of our family's new honesty policy, I will read it aloud."

JoAnne looked up sharply. "How do you know about the family's honesty stuff?"

"Remember when Aunt Mary said it," Charlie said. "And Aunt Penelope told us about Tabitha's real father, well, I was still Jane and invisible then, but I was in the room with Tabitha when you all were discussing it." She looked back at the paper.

Mary and JoAnne still appeared confused.

Dear Charlie,

I have made a number of grievous
mistakes in my life, but my greatest error
was in agreeing to stay out of your life.
Earlier, in my youth and desperation to
escape my family, I had surrendered my
DNA to my insane father and abandoned
my little sister to live alone in the Johnson
Family hell with him. In light of the
disaster my abandonment of my sister
caused, I should have been more sensitive
to my abandonment of you. I am
profoundly sorry for my complicity in that
decision. Neither your mother nor your
Aunt Mary ever knew this, but I saw you
the day you were born in the hospital. And
from that day on, for as long as I could still
walk, I followed your life. Whenever
possible, I would go watch you play in
your yard and watch you go to school. I
saw every one of your school graduations.
I saw you swim the breast stroke and win
for your swim team when you were seven.
I saw you play soccer for years before you
got to weak to play. In fact, I saw you play
your last soccer match where you
collapsed when you were in the eighth

grade. I saved your life as a diary and
picture album. I have an entire album of
the photos I took of you throughout your
life, hidden in my desk at home. I was
always so proud of you and the young lady
you were becoming. I had secret names for
both you and your sister. Yours was
Mookie and I called your sister Pookie. My
two daughters.

Charlie stopped reading and hid her face on
Darcy's shoulder, weeping. Through her own tears,
Darcy looked at her Mom and Aunt JoAnne. Both
were smiling and crying at the same time. They had
found chairs and were now sitting.

Darcy frowned with a flash of memory.
"Charlie, right before Dad died, he called me
Pookie but he also called out the name Mookie. I
didn't know what that meant until now."

Charlie took a ragged breath and raised her
head, smiling. She lifted the paper and continued to
read.

You have always been a strong, wonderful
person and I am proud to be able to help
you continue to live and grow, proud to
finally be able to make a real difference in
your life. Do not make the same mistakes I
made. Family can be difficult and painful,

but family is also precious and must be paramount. It is my dying wish that you and Darcy become, in life, the sisters you have always been, in blood. My wonderful daughter Charlie. I love you Mookie.

PS: Through my own actions, You and Darcy exist and I love you both. But, about thirteen years ago, I became aware of even more 'daughters', but not by my own actions. My father had my DNA used to inseminate my poor abused little sister in 2003. Then in 2005, two more church member's daughters were inseminated just before he died. All three of these young girls were abused for the purpose of trying to make more male Johnsons of my bloodlines using my DNA. I'd been looking for Penelope since 2004 and the other two since 2006, using a detective agency. I finally found Tabitha and Penelope in 2015. Please also welcome Tabitha as your sister into the family as well as your Aunt Penelope. I do not know where the other two sisters are. I hope you can find them one day. They are also innocent in all this.

Charlie looked at the attached photoshopped

image of Darcy and Charlie together when they were about twelve or thirteen, about the time when he had become bedridden. Handwritten across the bottom in her father's already unsteady script were the names, Mookie and Pookie.

Charlie hugged the note and photo smiling through her tears. Darcy hugged her and JoAnne hugged them both.

Mary jumped when her phone received another text from Penelope. She interpreted it aloud, "This one seems to be from Tabitha herself, she says please come to her room and save her from her Mother." Mary grinned and gestured toward JoAnne, who hesitated, looking back at Charlie.

"Mom. Go. I'm fine. I'll get a nurse to get more of these tubes out of me and I'll go see Tabitha too." Charlie waved her mother out. "Go help her."

Darcy stayed in Charlie's room, and Charlie started attacking the nurse call button until a nurse ran in, panic on her face.

"Nurse, please get me a gown, I've been naked long enough, and a wheelchair. I need to go see my other sister, Tabitha. And while you're at it, can you get this tube out of my vajayjay?"

The nurse laughed. "We'll see. I'll have to ask the doctor. First the gown and wheelchair. Those, we can do now."

Darcy pushed Charlie in her wheelchair into Tabitha's room. She was sitting up looking weak, but so much better. Penelope was still poking and prodding and checking her eyes. Tabitha was trying to avoid her Mother's intrusive hands as they kept pulling up the hospital gown and checking under it for marks. JoAnne and Mary were standing aside stifling their laughter and not helping at all.

Darcy rolled Charlie's chair to the bedside and interrupted. "Hello Tabitha, your two, long lost sisters have come to rescue you from your mother because your aunts are not helping at all."

She laughed weakly. "Please."

Penelope sighed and stepped aside, wiping her joyful tears, allowing Charlie's wheelchair closer. Darcy walked to the opposite bedside and Charlie stood up, holding onto the bed. Each took one of Tabitha's hands.

"Charlie! Sit down. It's way too early for you to be standing." JoAnne said.

"Mom, I'm find."

"Well, at least let me tie your gown together. Your mooning the entire world."

Charlie reached back to her butt. "Damn! I'm so used to the breezes. Gonna have to be more careful."

Tabitha looked closer at Charlie and then her brows raised and she smiled. "Jane? Is that you, all real now and not naked either."

"Yes, it's me. But my real name is Charlie. However, I do remember being Jane. And you guys have got to stop referring to me as naked." They all laughed.

Darcy said, "Tabitha, you are no longer alone. You have a mother, two aunts and the two of us, who are both actually your half-sisters. Turns out that Dad was Charlie's father too."

Charlie grinned. "I think we should just think of all three of us as regular sisters. Forget all that half stuff, our family has been split long enough. We are now two big sisters and a cute little sister."

Darcy tousled Tabitha's hair. "Yeah, little sister."

Tabitha forced a short chuckle, frowning. "Hey. Enough with the hair. Mom explained my Father to me after you left ... wait a minute. I'm not so little. I'm as tall as you guys already."

Charlie grinned. "Still, a little sister."

Mary cleared her throat. "Listen everybody. We three mothers now have three physically and mentally healthy children. We are a family and it's high time that we start acting like it. I think we should find a way to live together as a family. JoAnne, Penelope, over the next few days, lets talk and make some plans."

The three adults all nodded and Darcy grinned at Charlie and Tabitha. They all liked that idea as well.

CHAPTER TWENTY-ONE

After Darcy's mother and two aunts had firmly decided that all of them, adults and children, should live together as one big happy family in one house, she had felt a thrill course through her. Her new family would be striving to put aside their emotionally tortuous histories and just maybe, her father's death would be that catalyst, that driving force for the healing of her family. Darcy felt her life had more purpose and future, and she set herself to getting her life on tract so she could help all her new family.

Darcy had never been as busy as she became during the next two weeks after Charlie woke up and Jane disappeared for the last time. Her busy schedule started right away on Sunday, the very next day, as she caught her schoolwork up. She went to school early each day and worked to catch up on missed topics and take makeup tests. She withdrew from the cheerleading squad and the principal allowed her to leave school early each day after forth period to go to the hospital where she spent every afternoon with Charlie and Tabitha.

She also used her new driver's license to run errands for her mother and two aunts who were also spending as much time as possible at the hospital while also maintaining their jobs. She extended her visits most often through dinner, eating with her sisters and sometimes her aunts or mother, and going home just before bed.

Darcy's hospital time, from the awakenings on Saturday until Tuesday, ten days later, was mostly spent following both Charlie and Tabitha around to their various treatments, tests, and therapies. They were both improving unbelievably fast. Darcy was sure their dad was pleased that his organs had saved their lives but especially pleased that his family had also been saved and united.

Tabitha recovered her strength first and then joined Darcy as they both followed Charlie around on her therapy regimen, encouraging her performance. At least that's what they called it. Charlie complained loudly that their kibitzing was actually harassment.

They both cheered when Charlie's feeding tube and port were removed and the hole sutured up. But they laughed at Charlie's surprised whoop of discomfort when the urinary catheter was removed with a sudden sustained pull; whoosh. Charlie was still a little weak from being in a coma for three weeks, but PT was pleased with her progress in regaining her muscular strength. Her heart was performing perfectly with the carefully monitored cardio exercises.

Tuesday night of that second week, Darcy, Charlie, and Tabitha were eating dinner together in the hospital cafeteria while their mothers were each working late. They discussed the decision to all live together again and despite their enthusiastic approval for the idea, no one could conceive of how it could be accomplished. Though their official family relationship said they all were half-sisters sharing the same father, they felt like full sisters. They looked almost like triplets. Living together seemed such a natural thing and since Charlie and Tabitha were to be discharged on the coming Friday, time was of the essence.

Their conversation died as it did each time with no new ideas. After a few moments Tabitha frowned. "As I see it, we really have two problems; one right now, is where to live, but the other one has really been bothering me; this whole coma thing and Charlie's spirit. How could I see her, or you, Darcy. Was it father's organs that tied us together, or was it maybe sharing his DNA, or maybe both? Was it science or was something else working to finally bring our family together? Karma?"

Darcy frowned in thought. "Never thought about it like that. We don't know who got the other kidney or his lungs, but they're apparently okay. And we don't know anything about those other two 'sisters' he mentioned. Lets worry about where to live, first."

Charlie nodded in agreement. "Yeah, lets get a place to live first, but I am definitely interested in how that coma thing worked. I spent over three weeks as a naked spirit. I'd sure like to know why and how."

Tabitha nodded. "Well then, let's slow down and look at this logically. I like you guys and being sisters is cool. But, I ain't sharing a bed with either or both of you. Where could this many of us live? I live in a tiny apartment with only two bedrooms. And my little bed takes up most of my room."

"Same here," Charlie said. "Just a small apartment and only one bathroom, no shower, just a tub. And Darcy here is way too prudish to jump into the tub together with us, anyway."

"Shut up!" Darcy laughed. "You brazen hussy."

Tabitha looked back and forth between them, grinning. "You guys are funny ... weird, but funny. But, I ain't taking a bath with either one of you." She looked at Charlie. "And I would love to hear the real unabridged story of your free roaming naked spirit period."

"Sure," Charlie said. "But I wasn't free roaming. I pretty much was attached to Darcy and to my body like with a giant invisible rubber band. However, I want to forget the naked part."

Darcy nodded. "Good analogy. But back to the housing problem. My house is bigger but still too small for all of us." She shook her head in dismay until suddenly her eyes widened with shock. "But I do know of a place, a place that technically belongs to Charlie and I, sort of, the Baker Estate. But, that would mean moving to a new school district for all of us, a new community, and all new friends ... right in the middle of the school year."

Charlie nodded. "I remember parts of the discussion about the estate with you and your Mom when I was still invisible ..."

"And don't forget naked." Darcy interrupted, grinning.

"Shut up!" Charlie grimaced. "I really am trying to forget about that. Now, about moving, I had been sick so much before the transplant, that school and friends had already slipped away ... so moving is not an issue for me. Lets suggest it to our Moms."

Tabitha grinned. "Hey, Guys, don't forget me. I don't know what the 'Baker Estate' is, but I'm in the eighth grade. If the school system needed an enema, you would put it in at the eighth grade. I'm ready for a change. Tell me about this place."

"Let me text Mom first. She's at work, of course." Darcy took out her cellphone and texted her Mom about their idea and their feelings about moving in the middle of the school year. "Alright. Now we wait. Let's see, Tabitha. The Baker Estate is a large mansion and horse farm. They have a riding stable and also breed and train horses. My mom and Charlie's mom lived there as children until their parents died and they had to move in with relatives. Our grandparent's, in their will, gave it to any future grandchildren, Charlie and me, when we turn eighteen."

Mary texted back only a few minutes later. Darcy enlarged the screen and showed them her mom's message. "Great minds think alike. We had discussed that possibility previously but were unsure about how you guys would feel about a new school in the middle of the year. Glad you are okay with the move, as the Estate is the only place we can be together. We'll take care of the arrangements immediately. By the time Charlie and Tabitha are discharged at the end of the week, they will have a new home to go to! Professional movers will pack, move, and put away our stuff. Tell them just to relax and get better fast."

Darcy thought about her own school and friends. Changing schools and neighborhoods would be no problem for her, either. All her real friends, all two of them, were still in the hospital, hoping to get out by the end of the week. The others at her current school were more like acquaintances. Even leaving school now and missing that last week and a half before Christmas break would not be a problem. She would withdraw from school on Friday when Tabitha and Charlie were discharged.

Friday, December 7, finally arrived. But the hospital did not rush through the required discharge procedures in accordance with the level of their desire to leave. The nurses started with Tabitha and Penelope. After waiting for the nurses to finish all of their procedures and notes, they then waited for the doctors to review the nurses' notes and sign all their papers. Then they waited again for the nurses to revisit with Penelope and Tabitha and explain the doctor's discharge notes. Then they waited through the whole process again with JoAnne and Charlie.

It was almost three in the afternoon before they finally stood outside the hospital waiting for their ride. Mary and Darcy grinned at each other conspiratorially as they watched the others impatiently waiting for the transportation to arrive.

"I'm ready to get out of here. Where's that cab?" Tabitha said as she paced back and forth in front of the entrance.

Charlie stood by the curb, taking deep breaths of the cool air and just looked around, grinning. Darcy said, "Why are you grinning so big? You're just standing around out here and waiting like the rest of us."

"I'm just glad to be out of that damn bed." She patted her blouse and jeans. "And to be dressed."

Darcy and Tabitha laughed as Mary, JoAnne, and Penelope frowned. Within a few minutes, a long black limo pulled around and stopped in front of the entrance. The driver got out, walked around, and opened the wide passenger door. Except for Mary and Darcy, they all stepped back out of the way and looked back at the hospital entrance, expecting an important boarding party. They saw no one.

The driver announced, "The Baker party, the Winters party, and the Johnson party, your car is ready."

Charlie and Tabitha's mouths dropped open and they stopped talking. Darcy laughed as she ushered them into the limo. The adults followed, Mary smiling broadly as she guided the other two into the limo. The mothers took seats on the rear bench seat, while Darcy, Charlie, and Tabitha plopped down in the individual bucket seats.

Mary looked at Darcy and grinned. "Told you."

JoAnne shook her head. "You and Darcy knew about this. I can't believe you managed to keep it a secret."

"Well, I think this is great. Never been in a limo before," Tabitha said as she felt the leather upholstery.

"Me neither." Charlie looked at Darcy from under lowered brows. "You knew about this and you didn't tell us. You jerk."

Darcy look down her nose at the other two. "Well, as the oldest, it was my job to bring some dignity to our wait and our ride."

Mary grinned and shook her head as she picked up her phone. She selected a video. "Here girls, watch this. This is my oh-so-cool daughter, Darcy, when she found out about the limo ride." They all watched Darcy leaping, twirling, and whooped loudly in her nightie, forgetting entirely about her lack of proper attire. Darcy sat quietly, chastened, for the next few minutes.

The driver announced that the ride should take approximately forty-five minutes and they were welcome to the refreshments available. Most of the remaining travel time was filled with quiet conversations between the adults, and chewing and slurping from the girls.

The sounds of eating were replaced with oohing and aahing as the limo entered the driveway, rounded the fountain, and stopped under the porte cochere. Tabitha giggled as she waited for the driver to open their door. A man in a black suit stepped down from the grand entrance steps and said. "Welcome home, Mrs. Winters, Miss. Baker. It has been many years."

"Robeson!" Mary said smiling from ear to ear. She and JoAnne both stepped forward and briefly embraced him. Other than a smile, he remained straight and proper. Mary gestured to Penelope. "This is my sister-in-law Penelope Johnson and her daughter Tabitha, and these are JoAnne's and my daughters, Charlie and Darcy. Penelope is a sister to me and JoAnne."

"I understand." Robeson said with a nod. "Welcome Miss. Johnson and welcome young ladies. Please follow me. Call me Robeson. I am the Estate Manager and in charge of all the staff working on the Baker Estate. Estelle, whom you shall meet later, is my second, in charge of the household staff. Gustavo, likewise, is my second, in charge of the staff who care for the animals and the grounds."

Robeson lead them up a grand stairway into the center wing of the mansion. Darcy, Charlie, and Tabitha looked back and forth between themselves as they walked, all unusually silent. He stopped and pointed to a door. "Mrs. Winters, this is the Baker Suite consisting of three bedrooms, each with a private bath and a shared common sitting room. Your belongings have already been distributed. The Thompson Suite at the end of the hall is for the young ladies."

Darcy, Charlotte, and Tabitha ran past him into their shared common sitting room and began exploring. The girl's suite had four bedrooms, a long shared balcony, a common lounging area, and a single, but enormous bathroom. All their things were already in place in three of the bedrooms. There was nothing for them to do but begin to individualize their personal belongings in their own styles.

A formal dinner was served in the main dining room in celebration of Charlie's and Tabitha's release from the Hospital, followed by an evening spent watching movies in the home theater. Before bed, Darcy, Charlie, and Tabitha sat on their balcony and talked late into the night, too keyed up to sleep. Their mothers had retired much earlier as they were going to return to work in the morning and the drive was now much longer.

CHAPTER TWENTY-TWO

The girls knew their moms didn't really need to work for financial reasons any more, but they understood their need to get out of the house. After breakfast, served in their common room, they decided to get out of the house, themselves, and explore the estate. They hiked the fields and forest, swam in the pool, and played tennis on the courts. Darcy and Charlie tried riding horses for the very first time accompanied by Tabitha' laughter at their antics. She had experience with horses from living on the farm in Missouri.

That night at dinner, the mothers talked about their work as the girls looked back and forth, grimacing. JoAnne and Penelope delved deep into the intricacies of computer network installation after Penelope informed them that she was a coder and worked for a software development firm. She had been on sick child leave since Tabitha had been hospitalized.

"Mom," Charlie said. "Sorry to interrupt, but can we talk about something else. We would rather watch old trucks rust than hear about network installation and service."

"What a sarcastic smart a ... lec you are, my dearest daughter." JoAnne said. "You have a more interesting topic in mind?"

"Well, we've been thinking. We all three ran and walked and swam and played tennis and other sporty things all day. It was great. I feel like ... no, I am a new person. When school starts for us in January, I want to play soccer again, Tabitha and Darcy too, okay?"

"We'll have to get your doctor's okay but I am so glad you're feeling better." JoAnne said. "It's been a number of years since you've had the energy."

Mary looked at Darcy and Tabitha. "You guys too?"

Darcy and Tabitha confirmed their desires to play soccer, and while Tabitha and Charlie talked of soccer, Darcy's mind wandered.

She watched her family as her mother, her mother's sister and sister-in-law talked, coming to an agreement about the girls' future in school sports. The two sisters and sister-in-law were just three sisters, for all practical purposes. Darcy smiled, feeling wonderful, warm, and not alone any more. She had come from a family with only a mother to a family with three mothers and two sisters.

She glanced around her new family. It was a strange household. It seemed to have three children; sisters, two older sisters and a younger sister who didn't act all that much younger. Then there were three mothers who were also sisters. It was cool to have two sisters, but having three moms was weird. Mary, seemed to be the chief mom, maybe because she was oldest.

Darcy's mother sighed like she does when something weighty needs saying. "We three, your mothers, had actually discussed this previously. While you are all on this extended vacation till you start your new schools in January, you can fill your time with sports and other physical activities in moderation. But when school starts, it's academics first then maybe sports. Remember, it's a new school system with new expectations and it may take a while to make the adjustments."

"Mom. We understand that." Darcy looked at Charlie and Tabitha. "Right?" They all nodded like bobble-heads, three tall, red headed, green eyed sisters, looking like triplets. Darcy's eyes got big with excitement. "Mom! I just had a thought. Charlie and Tabitha are also grandchildren. This will all be ours when we turn eighteen."

Mary stopped eating and looked at JoAnne and

Penelope, who had resumed discussing the network and had missed Darcy statement. "JoAnne! Penelope! Listen. Something needs discussion and clarification."

Darcy grinned at Charlie and Tabitha but spoke to her mother. "Wow, Mom. You sound like a big sister ... well, a much older, big sister."

Mary grinned. "Enough with that 'older' stuff. I'm still your mother and don't you forget it."

The others looked up from their conversation and Mary nodded at Darcy. "Now, what was that thought again, Darcy?"

"I was just commenting that we three grandchildren," she pointed at herself, Charlie, and Tabitha. "Will inherit the mansion when we are eighteen."

"Not precisely accurate." Mary said. "First, the estate and property is in trust for the grandchildren of George Thompson Baker and Matilda Abigail Baker. That is you and Charlie. But course, when it is yours, if you wish to share the ownership with the other known children in your family, like Tabitha, it would be your right. But if you wanted to share this mansion with all the children of your generation, remember, there are two more, according to your father."

Darcy sat up straight and looked at her sisters. "I guess we'll have time to solve the mansion thing in a few years then. But right now, we have a mystery to solve. There are two other half sisters, somewhere ... and we haven't done any searching for them, but Dad already seemed to know some very specific things about them. I wonder if it was from that detective agency he mentioned. Maybe there is info in his old desk where he seemed to hide everything else."

Charlie brightened. "Yeah, we still haven't looked for that picture album of me, the one his note talked about."

JoAnne smiled. "Your Father's desk was moved into the library on the first floor, untouched and still locked."

Mary sighed. "We have not had the time or the will to dig through it yet, but you three have our permission. The key is in my purse upstairs." She pointed up toward her suite.

Darcy, Charlie, and Tabitha excused themselves and ran to get the key, leaving their mothers to their boring work conversations. The library occupied the rear area of the first floor of the center wing of the mansion, with massive windows looking out over a hundred acre pasture with grazing horses. Their father's desk stood near the windows, its computer and video equipment already wired up. But they ignored the electronics except for a few longing glances by both Charlie and Tabitha.

In the left-hand file drawer, under the hanging

files, they found a false bottom which opened with the desk key to reveal Charlie's photo album, a purple file folder labeled "Barbosa Detective Agency", and a sealed envelope addressed to Tabitha.

Charlie took her album but didn't open it, holding it against her chest instead. Her expression vacillated between joy and fear as she sank to the floor, her back against the side of the desk. Darcy picked up the detective folder and handed the envelope to Tabitha, who slid down the side of the desk beside Charlie. Darcy sat on the floor in front of her sisters. "Okay guys, let's open 'em."

Tabitha held her envelope by its corner like it could bite as she leaned her head back against the desk, her eyes closed. "Charlie, you first. At least you already knew that the album was there, I'm not sure what I have and I'm a little afraid to find out."

"This album is just pictures of me growing up, proof that dad ... uh ... well, I want to share it with Mom first. You go ahead." Charlie patted Tabitha's knee reassuringly. Tabitha looked at Darcy who nodded enthusiastically.

"Okay." Tabitha said, holding the envelope out from her and slowly prying the sealed flap loose. She pulled out a folded piece of paper filled with printing.

"Well, don't just look at it. Go ahead and read it," Charlie said. "He left me a message as well. It'll be good."

Tabitha unfolded the note but still did not look at it. "You know, I never questioned the fact that I didn't have a father until I got into school. After hearing the other kids talk of their fathers, I would ask Mom about my father and she would get so embarrassed and upset. Eventually, I just stopped asking. Later, when I understood more about sex and stuff, I figured she had been raped and my father was some kind of evil bastard. So, I just stopped thinking about it. Then, a couple of weeks ago, after I woke up in the hospital, Mom explained about the artificial insemination with Dad's sperm. I guess in a way she was raped. But my ... our father, was also a victim and not evil. What does that make me? Don't know how I feel about that. My father was also my uncle ... but guess that's better than the story that grandfather raped her. Then my mother would also have been my sister."

"That confusing," Darcy said. "Look, we're your sisters. We have the same dad. We are sharing our three Moms ... strange but true. You have a family that loves you. Read the damn note before the paper disintegrates from age."

Tabitha grinned and began to read.

Dear Tabitha,
I'm sorry that I was unable to give you this note in person. I had been hunting for you

and your mother since she, my little sister, disappeared in 2004. I only became aware of your location the year I became bedridden, in 2015. The detective agency I hired had worked tirelessly from 2004, until 2015 when they finally located you and your mother. You where discovered on that cursed unwed mother's farm in Missouri, where your mother had been sent by our insane father. I contacted her and told her of my illness and that she should come to the Santa Monica area. I sent money for your move and I paid for you to go to a good private school to help you catch up from the poor education you had been offered on the farm.

But I knew I could not bring Mary or JoAnne around to interacting with your mother at that time, so I never told them that I had found you and your mother. I know they are both good people and will eventually change their minds. Sorry, I couldn't follow your life after I found you, but I was already under life support by the time you moved to this area.

I wish I had been a better brother to your mother and I wish I could have been the father you deserved in your life. Please understand and try to forgive our family for our mistakes. Please try to make our family work. Don't let the past mistakes of the adults keep our family apart.

Love, Your Father

She dropped the note into her lap and wiped her tears. "I wish I had known him." She folded the note and stuffed it into her pocket. "What's in the detective's folder?"

Darcy paraphrased from the report. "This first sheet detailed the location of the first child, our little sister Tabitha here. The second sheet explains the work, to date, on the other two daughters. Seems that they both had been born in 2006, after the ... our grandfather had died. Their mothers had been unwilling to raise the children under the circumstances and they both had been passed around within the congregation for almost six years like an unofficial foster care. But without the presence of our grandfather, they were eventually released into the official foster care system in Boulder City, Nevada."

Darcy looked up from her reading. "Guys, listen to this. Both of the now twelve year old girls have curly red hair and green eyes and are tall for their age. They had just been transferred to foster care in Las Vegas when this report was written.

"Passed around the congregation. That doesn't

sound good." Charlie said as she helped Tabitha up from the floor.

"Foster care in Las Vegas." Tabitha said. "Not good either."

"We need more sisters, right?" Charlie nodded vigorously.

"Yeah, some actual 'little sisters'," Tabitha said, laughing.

"Well, lets talk to our mothers about it tomorrow." Darcy said. "It's already late."

The next morning at breakfast, the triumvirate of Mothers agreed to seek the remaining two sisters and offer adoption. Mary, as the widow of the man who had contracted with them for so many years, called the detective agency right from the table She asked them to complete their work and locate the names and specific location for each girl. Then she went silent for a moment, listening. Her eyes widened in surprise, she thanked them, and ended the call.

Mary laid her phone down and sighed. "What is it about this family. JoAnne and I think our older, criminal sister killed our parents. Your father had two children by different women and then three more because of his insane father. Then to make it worse, JoAnne and I went a little crazy with jealousy and anger" She looked at Tabitha. "Sorry. That sounded bad. You know he would have loved you, had he been physically able."

"I know. He left me a note." She passed it around to the mothers.

"I had no idea that he was looking for you all those years. He never said anything until 2018 when you got sick." Mary shook her head and looked at Tabitha and JoAnne. "And he knew about the other two from the beginning too."

JoAnne sighed. "His silence was our fault. We made him promise some terrible things but he did his best to be a good man and father despite us. Let's complete his wishes. Mary. What did the agency say before you hung up?"

"They said they had already completed their investigation but when your father died, they had no one to provide the results to." Mary said and shrugged, then smiled wryly.

The three girls sat at the edge of their seats waiting for Mary to continue until Tabitha let out her held breath explosively. "I'm running out of air, waiting. What did they say?"

Mary laughed and explained the detective agency's latest results. "As part of the agency's first set of inquiries, they had informed the Las Vegas foster care system that the girls' biological father was seeking them from Santa Monica. Somehow, both girls had found this out, about their own sisterhood and their shared father. Two weeks ago, they had run away together, planning to come to Santa Monica to find their father."

Mary shook her head sadly. "But they had not heard that Gary had died and there had been no information on them until last week. Both girls had been found by the Santa Monica police living in the water drainage system with some homeless people, ill from malnutrition and exposure. They had been taken to the hospital in a semiconscious state as Jane Does and they both slipped in light comas. They were subsequently identified from their descriptions, but remain in the hospital due to their condition, the local hospital, here in Santa Monica."

"Here?" Darcy said. "I can't believe it."

"After lunch today, we'll go visit them," Mary said. "But we'll probable have to wait till Monday to make what arrangements are needed with social services."

The day was beautiful for the middle of December and warm enough to go swimming. All three girls spent the next three hours at the pool and then returned to get ready to visit the two girls in the hospital. They cleaned up, dressed and flopped down on the lounge chairs in the TV room to wait for their mothers to finish getting ready.

With no warning of any kind, two naked, red haired, green eyed, girls about twelve years old, appeared sitting on the sofa covering themselves with her hands and crying. They looked at each other and then at Darcy, Charlie, and Tabitha. "Who are they? Where are we?"

"Charlie, Tabitha, Tell me your seeing this too?" Darcy said.

"Damn! They're naked!" Tabitha said. The two young girls looked at her in shock.

"You can see us?"

"Jeez, not again!" Charlie said.

"Mom!" All three shouted together."

END

Thank you for reading my book. If you enjoyed it, won't you please take a moment to leave me a review where you purchased it?

Thanks!

F. Hampton Carmine

About The Author

Hampton Carmine has been writing stories since high school in the early sixties when he completed three sci/fi novels that still exist in red ink on pulp pencil tablets, kept as instruments of humility.

He was born in the small college town of Oakland City, Indiana where his dad was in music school. His youth was spent in the mid-west but he went to college in North Carolina at East Carolina University achieving a degree in Psychology and advanced degrees in Speech and Language Pathology and Special Education. This was followed later by a degree in Computer Science, a career in state service and retirement to help raise a first grandchild.

He continues to write Fantasy and Sci/Fi as well as compose music for band and orchestra while living in Raleigh, NC.

Also by F. Hampton Carmine
All Available in eBook & Print versions
on Amazon.com

Novels:

The Star Mark, Book 1, The Dragons' Gift Trilogy
Abby and the Magic Key
Rebecca Hornsby, Elf Princess
Destiny's Handmaiden
April Showers, Failed Fairy
Teela of Kolander
Katrina's Journey: Discovery
Katrina's Journey: Evolution

Short Stories:

Bright Eyes
It's For Your Own Good
Man - Machine: A Journey, Three Short Stories
The Return of Princess Moonbeam Broadwing
The Seer, Destiny's Guardian
A Matter of Faith
The Burning Bush Redux
Ghost Story
The Gluon Amplifier
Throwback
Written in Her Flesh
A Gift of Butterflies
He Who Saves a Single Life, Saves ... World Entire
A Matter of Perspective
The Bone Reader
Standoff at Europa
The Harpist of Souls
Ride the High Air
Hurting

Connect With Me:

Check out my Website:
http://www.hamptoncarmine.com

Friend me on Facebook:
http://facebook.com/HamptonCarminesStories

Find me on Amazon:
http://www.amazon.com
(search for Hampton Carmine)

CPSIA information can be obtained
at www.ICGtesting.com
Printed in the USA
LVHW081729201120
672263LV00031B/1297